The /

MW00881879

Written by
James M. Corkill.

Chapter 1

GROOM LAKE, NEVADA:

The special jet stopped in front of the security checkpoint, and Alex looked out the window as an unmarked vehicle drove up and stopped next to the plane. A knot formed in his stomach as he released his seatbelt and stood to grab his backpack. The attendant indicated for him to leave it on the plane, and then she opened the exit door and lowered the stairs. He slowly descended the steps and stopped in front of two armed men dressed in suits and ties. "What's going on?"

"I'm Secret Service Agent Garcia, and we have orders to escort you to Director Blake's office. Get in, please."

Alex did as instructed and climbed into the back seat, and they drove past the security guards. They stopped in front of the admin building, and everyone climbed out then Alex led the way inside and down the hallway to Holly's office. The door was open, so Alex stepped into the room, noticing the two agents remained in the hallway. He saw Holly sitting in a chair behind her desk, and a tall, masculine looking woman dressed in a US Air Force Captain's uniform standing beside her.

His heart raced when he saw young Jadin Avery standing to one side of the room. She was part of his team, and he hoped she was not in trouble as he turned to Holly. "What's going on, Director?"

"This is Captain Sharon Fargo. It seems our new President wants the military to take over operation of your spacecraft, and she's in charge of the first training program."

Alex stared at Fargo. "That ship belongs to me, and the government can't just take it."

Fargo moved around the desk and locked stares with Alex. "It's done. Live with it."

Alex's hands clenched into fists as he turned to look at Holly. "You can't let them get away with this." The look in Holly's eyes told him she had no choice, so he turned back to Fargo. "On whose authority?"

Fargo grabbed a folder on the desk and held it out to Alex. "This is from the Attorney General, granting me the authority to claim the ship under the law of Eminent Domain. Meaning, if it's for the good of the country, the government can take your spaceship."

Alex didn't take the folder and stared into Fargo's eyes. "Over my dead body!"

"I hope it doesn't come to that, Mister Cave."

"What about my team?"

"Since Jadin officially works for NASA, she will teach us how to operate the spacecraft. I'm sure we can get by without you, so I revoke your security clearance and my people will escort you back to the plane. Your belongings in your apartment will be shipped to your designated location."

Jadin saw the rage in Alex's expression and his clenched fists, and wanted him to shut up before he got into more trouble, so she grabbed Fargo's arm to get her attention away from him. "I think I can work with you on this, Captain Fargo. How about I start the training on Monday morning? That gives me three days to shut down my research project at the Jet Propulsion Laboratory in Pasadena."

Fargo tossed the folder onto the desk. "That's fine."

When Jadin saw Fargo indicate for her men to get Alex back to the jet, she reached up to wrap her arms around his neck, pulling him close for a hug. "Call me later, okay?"

Alex put his cheek against hers so he could whisper into her ear. "This isn't over."

Jadin noticed Fargo staring at them and slowly raised her hands up to Alex's face. She cupped them over his ears to pull him close, covertly inserting a communication device into his right ear. "I have an idea, so don't do anything rash. I'll explain later."

When Jadin gave him a soft kiss on his lips and stepped back, Alex reached across the desk to shake Holly's hand. "It's been nice working with you, Director."

Holly didn't accept, and walked around the desk to give him a hug. When he bent down, she turned to him so Fargo could not see her face, and whispered in his ear. "I'll keep you updated on what happens here."

"Don't get in trouble over me."

Holly let go and stepped back. "Stay safe."

Fargo saw the moisture building up in Jadin's eyes. "Am I going to have any problems with you, Ms. Avery?"

Jadin wanted to tell her where to shove her problems, but her self-restraint won. "No, Captain. I'll meet with your astronauts at Hangar 5 first thing Monday morning."

Fargo indicated the doorway to Alex. "After you, Mister Cave."

Alex reluctantly left with the two men for the flight back to Las Vegas. Jadin stepped into the hallway and stared after Alex, finding it hard to believe he was leaving for good. She felt Fargo's hand on her shoulder and moved back into the room then folded her arms across her chest and stared at the Captain. "What about David? He can help."

"Mister Conway no longer works here and left four days ago."

Jadin's jaw hung open as her arms dropped to her sides. "That's ridiculous. He's the only person who knows how the engine works and needs to be here, too."

Holly locked stares with Fargo. "She's correct. If you have any problems, you'll need his help."

"I'll call him in as an advisor if necessary. I'll expect daily reports on the program's progress, Ms. Blake." She spun around and headed out of the room toward the exit.

Jadin gave Holly a troubled expression. "I don't think this will work. Even if I show Fargo's people how to use the ship, Melvin, the ship's AI, won't follow their commands."

"Will he follow yours?"

Jadin thought about it for a moment. "I have no idea."

Holly moved around the desk to sit in her chair. "I'm worried about David. Fargo was less than subtle when she fired him, and he took it hard. I haven't been able to contact him since he left the base."

"I'll try to locate him."

"All right. When will you leave for JPL?"

Jadin suddenly realized she could ride with Alex to Las Vegas. "Right now. I don't need to pack anything, so I'll ride with Alex. I'd better hurry, so I'll see you on Sunday afternoon."

"Wait a minute. I know how you feel about Alex, but you need to let him go. At least for now. Fargo will be on that flight and we don't want her thinking there is a conspiracy between you two. The plane will be back in an hour, so take care of things here before you leave."

Jadin realized Holly was correct. "All right. What do you know about my feelings for Alex?"

"That he thinks you two can't be lovers and work together."

"Is it that obvious?"

"To me, yes, but I can't speak for anyone else."

"At least that won't be a problem anymore. I'll start packing Alex's personal items in his room while I wait. I'll see you when I get back."

Holly leaned back in her chair and stared after Jadin. "This should get interesting."

Chapter 2

ANACORTES MARINA, WASHINGTON STATE, USA:

Alex stepped out from the Harbormaster's office, where he had received a key to the *Mystic's* motorboat. He strolled along the floating concrete docks, admiring the pleasure crafts in the uncovered mooring slips. He acknowledged a few people relaxing on a large sailboat and yearned to be on the water again. As he passed the stern of a forty-foot cabin cruiser, he received flirtatious smiles from two women in skimpy swimsuits. He indicated he appreciated the offer, but continued along the mooring spaces.

He looked out across the water and recognized the *Mystic*; a two-hundred and fifty foot tri-hull research ship anchored in the harbor. The sweptback design of her blue and white hull was graceful and aerodynamic, ending with an open stern deck for a nineteen foot motorboat, a fifteen foot submarine, and a six-person helicopter. It belonged to millionaire scientist and researcher Mike Tanner, a long-time friend who had called him two hours ago asking for his help, so he left his family ranch in Sparrow Valley for a face-to-face conversation.

He recognized the *Mystic's* motorboat tied to the dock, so he climbed in and started the engine. Once the ropes were untied from the cleats, he backed out of the slip and drove toward the open water. He continued past the Mystic's bow and recognized the tri-hull design, with the two outside pontoons housing the electric motors and the water jet pumps. They were powered by twin turbine engines driving the generators in the main body of the ship.

When he reached the *Mystic's* stern deck, he looked up at the man coming down the outside stairs from the bridge. "Hey, Mike. Permission to come aboard?"

Mike smiled and strolled across the deck, then reached out to shake Alex's hand. "Granted. Sorry to take you away from your family visit, but I'm glad you could make it."

Alex looked down at the five-foot-nine, sixty-year-old man with graying brown hair. "No problem, Mike. It's only an hour's drive, and I'm currently unemployed."

Mike was one of the few people who knew about Alex's work at Area 51. "When did that happen?"

"Two days ago. The government took Melvin from me."

Mike's jaw dropped open as he stared at Alex. "They took your spacecraft? How can they get away with that? I was there when you found it in that volcano, so I'm a witness if you need me to testify."

"The President's representative is claiming Eminent Domain."

"That's a bunch of crap. Let's go inside and I'll show you why I called."

Alex followed Mike into the ship to the lounge and dining area, and then they sat down at a large wooden table. "Where's the rest of the crew?"

Mike set his briefcase down, then opened it and reached inside to retrieve a few photographs. "They're taking a few days of personal time. We just got back from spending a month investigating a series of unexplained seismic phenomena. As you know, there has been a significant increase in the number of tsunamis lately along the North Pacific Rim. From the information I've gathered so far, I believe the Tamu Massif is the epicenter of the seismic events causing the waves."

Alex grabbed a photograph and saw a picture of the underwater volcano. "That massif has been dead for a million years. But it's also the intersection of three tectonic plates, so something must be causing them to shift."

Mike slid another image to Alex. "You're correct, and I think I know what's causing it. Our underwater drone took this picture two weeks ago while we were searching the waters around the volcano."

Alex studied the image. "It looks like an oval circle of stone on the seabed. What are the dimensions?"

"Eighty feet at the widest point and one hundred feet long. We set up a grid of sensors to monitor the area remotely, and just before we got up to speed, we received data showing a four-point-six seismic event. We stopped, and that's when we detected a strange sound on our sonar."

"Aftershocks?"

"No, it was mechanical. The sound continued for several minutes and we determined it came from the oval rock. When the sound stopped, we went back to investigate, but we didn't pick it up again. We sent the drone back down and saw this. Does it look familiar?"

When Mike slid another image across to him, Alex studied the magnified view of a small section of a mirrored surface. "It's just like the exterior of my spaceship."

"Yes, and I believe that is causing the seismic events. What has me concerned is the last four earthquakes were exactly seventy-eight hours apart, and increasing in magnitude. We're headed back to the volcano, and I was hoping you'd like to join us."

Mike noticed the sparkle of excitement in Alex's eyes when he smiled back at him. "I take that as a yes."

"I just need to say goodbye to my family first. When are you leaving?"

"My ship is ready whenever you are, and the crew can be back in about four hours, if that's not too soon."

Alex stood from the table. "That would be fine, Mike."

Alex followed him out to the stern and climbed into the motorboat, then started the engine and looked at his friend, removing the rope from the cleat. "I'll see you here this afternoon."

"The crew will be glad to see you again. Just leave the key in the office."

Alex shoved the boat away from the stern, then put the engine in gear and steered toward the dock. He looked back over his shoulder and saw Mike talking on his phone, then turned back and grinned, knowing it was the start of a new adventure.

***

THE *MYSTIC*:

Alex moved to the railing behind the bridge and looked down at the *Wizard*, a fifteen foot long, white and light blue submarine, which was cradled in a storage bracket on the left side of the stern. He felt a slight adrenaline rush at the prospect of a new mystery to solve with his friends.

He glanced at Mike, who moved up beside him at the railing. "Where's the helicopter?"

"The Marina won't let Bett land on the ship while we're in the harbor, so she'll catch up with us in the Strait of Juan de Fuca."

Mike waved down at the six-foot-one, physically fit blond man checking the hold-down straps on the motorboat below. Francis Okawna, (O'Conna), was the thirty-five-year-old chief engineer and sub operator, and Alex's best friend.

Okawna hurried up the outside stairs to the lookout deck outside the bridge and stopped near Mike and Alex. "We're ready."

Mike stepped onto the bridge and looked at the man standing at the helm. At six foot six inches and sporting a thick red beard, Joshua Mason appeared more like a lumberjack with a baritone voice than a computer and electronic genius.

"We're ready to get underway, Josh."

Joshua smiled. "This should be a fun trip."

With Okawna and Alex as spotters, Josh used the directional thrusters to spin the *Mystic* around in a stationary circle and then headed out into the Strait of Juan de Fuca. He was looking forward to his wife and childhood sweetheart, Bett, a five-foot-six-inch blond woman and the helicopter pilot, returning from visiting her family.

***

Bett Mason cruised along in her blue and white helicopter with the waters of the strait sliding beneath her. Up ahead, she saw the outline of a sleek-looking tri-hauled ship, and then lined up with the stern. She set the helicopter down on the fifty foot wide deck then shut down the engines and climbed out.

She saw Alex and Okawna step out from the doors in the forward bulkhead, so she went over and reached up to give Alex a hug. "Welcome back."

Alex bent over to wrap his arms around her shoulders. "It's nice to see you again, too."

When she let go, he watched her jog up the stairs to join Joshua on the bridge, then turned when he heard Okawna's voice. "What was that?"

"Give me a hand with the helicopter, buddy, so we can get underway. Once we reach open water, we'll get up to full speed and we should reach the massif in forty-eight hours."

Alex grabbed the tie-down straps and quickly secured the helicopter to the deck, then stared up at Okawna, who was folding the blades back over the tail rotor. He admired how the ship and all its toys were aerodynamic and state-of-the-art.

Once Okawna climbed down, he led Alex up the steps and onto the bridge. "We're all set, Josh."

When Josh pressed a button, Alex grabbed the handrail as the *Mystic* quickly got up to her full cruising speed of seventy-eight knots per hour. If the radar detected any approaching vessels, the automated avoidance system would take control, but someone would always be on watch for the unexpected.

***

TAMU MASSIF:

Okawna checked the gauges inside the submarine one last time and everything was as it should be. "*Mystic*, this is the *Wizard*. We're going down."

Okawna looked into the rearview mirror above the bubble window in the sub's nose and saw Alex sitting directly behind him. "If that object down there is a spaceship, I hope it's not occupied."

Alex knew how Okawna felt. They had met four different races of humans, and one of them wasn't friendly.

He felt the G-force as Okawna engaged the rear thruster, and then they were finally underway. He took a moment to admire the walls of the mini-sub, but this was not his first time inside, and he knew it was made from a high-tech form of ceramic, capable of withstanding immense pressure.

The sub leveled out, and he looked at Okawna's reflection in the mirror. "I forgot to ask. How deep are we going?"

"About two miles."

With fifteen minutes of dive time to kill, they reminisced about their time together as CIA operatives in Russia, and Alex still mourned the murder of his new wife in Holland eight years ago. It was the reason he quit, and he'd be dead right now if Okawna hadn't smuggled him out of Europe.

Alex noticed a change in their direction, and then the powerful lights from the sub illuminated a thirty-foot area of exposed alien technology. He leaned forward over Okawna's shoulder to stare through the front window as the sub headed toward the massive, mirrored surface.

"That's incredible, Okawna."

The sub stopped within a foot of the alien object and Alex studied the smooth surface of the exposed section, which disappeared under the silt. "I don't see any scratch marks, and it appears to be unaffected by the seismic activity. Are you recording this?"

"Yeah, since we arrived. Let's see if we can find some kind of seam that might indicate an entrance. Too bad you don't have your spaceship anymore. Melvin might know how to get inside."

"You're right. Jadin is supposed to train the astronauts today, and if they're in orbit, I might be able to talk to him once we're on the surface."

Alex had an idea perhaps the ancient technology might be compatible with Melvin's technology, so he slid the small communication device Jadin gave him into his ear and turned it on. "Hello. Can anyone hear me?"

A section of the alien object suddenly split down the center, and the two thirty-foot sections disappeared. The sub was suddenly surrounded by a bubble of gas rising from the structure, and without the supporting water, the sub dropped into the opening. Alex grabbed the back of Okawna's seat with both hands, expecting to crash, but the water rushed in to fill the void, engulfing the small craft and creating lift just before it slammed onto the floor of the object.

When the water stopped moving, Alex let go of Okawna's seat. "Can anyone hear me?"

Okawna aimed one of the exterior lights at the wall and saw a pewter color and then tilted the nose of the sub down and saw the bottom of the chamber. "It's about thirty feet deep. What do you think it is?"

"It's hard to say, but something responded to my radio signal. Swing us around and let's see where we are."

The sub spun in a stationary circle, with the lights reflecting off the curved interior of the chamber. It was a sixty-foot diameter symmetrical hole with nothing in the center.

Alex noticed a thin, eight foot tall seam in the wall. "That could indicate the entrance into this object."

"Yeah, but even our best diving suits can't withstand the pressure at this depth. We can't get inside."

Alex leaned back in his seat. "You might as well take us back to the *Mystic* until we decide how to proceed."

Okawna drove the sub up out of the opening and slowly turned in a circle to check out any changes. The churning water had dislodged sediment, which exposed more of the mirrored surface. "Is that what I think it is? Because it looks way too big to be a spaceship."

Alex studied the massive oval mirror poking through the surface of the seafloor. "It's hard to say without seeing the rest of it."

Okawna steered the sub in a wide circle around the alien object as they slowly rose through the water. When the light from the sub no longer reached the seafloor, he pointed the front toward the *Mystic* and sped up for their return to the surface.

***

Mike was on the rear deck area of the ship, watching Josh operate the hoist, which was raising the submarine from the ocean. He stepped out of the way when water splattered across the deck as the *Wizard* swung around onto its storage bracket, then he walked with Bett to the side of the sub.

Mike leaned a fiberglass ladder against the side of the small craft and then turned to Bett. "I'm always relieved when the sub returns. Even with the most modern equipment, there is always the possibility something could go wrong."

Okawna was on his way down the ladder when he heard Mike's comment. "Yeah, but not this time. It's another spaceship."

Once Alex climbed down the ladder and joined the group, Mike indicated the door in the rear bulkhead and headed that way, with Alex at his side. "Is it like your ship?"

"I'm not so sure. Okawna recorded everything, so you'll see in a moment."

When they entered the lounge, Alex grabbed the digital storage device from his pocket and gave it to Josh. A moment later, a still image appeared on the large monitor mounted to the forward bulkhead.

The recording started with a view from the nose of the submarine as Alex narrated. "As you can see, the surface appears to be the same material as my ship."

The image suddenly became blurry for a few seconds. "That happened when I tried to contact Melvin. A section of the top near the end opened, and we dropped into the chamber. The radio signal must have caused it to react."

The recording showed the sub turning in a circle, then rising out of the room. As the sub gained altitude, everyone saw the opening into the object was a sixty-foot diameter hole, thirty feet deep.

When the recording stopped, Alex looked at his friends. "Perhaps Melvin knows something about it. Too bad he doesn't belong to me anymore."

Okawna saw the dejected expression in Alex's eyes. "I'm sure once Holly learns about this new discovery, you'll get your job back."

"I don't think so. Holly's not in charge anymore, and Captain Fargo will want to take over the operation."

He had an idea and looked at Mike. "I'm sure you know, according to Maritime Law, the alien structure belongs to you, so I'll let you decide if we should inform the authorities about it."

Mike stared at Alex for a moment. "I get the feeling you don't want me to."

"You're correct. We both know how a discovery of this magnitude will create a political nightmare for all nations. Right now, it belongs to you, and no one else knows about it. In my opinion, you're the best person to be in control of this advanced technology. You're honest and smart, and not prone to making rash decisions."

Mike thought about it for a moment. "I can't make a decision of this magnitude until I know what it is. The only way to do that is with your spaceship, and you'll need government approval. You were just fired, so I don't see where I have a choice."

Alex gave Mike a smirk. "I have another idea. A friend of ours might have just what we need to get inside that structure, but we'll also need your resources."

Mike had worked with Alex enough to trust his ideas. "All right. What do you need from me?"

"A plane ride to Fallon, Nevada."

Mike looked over at Bett. "Can your helicopter make it to a military base on one of the Aleutian Islands?"

Bett shook her head no. "I was studying the charts while on the bridge. It's just too far, but Japan is within my range."

Mike turned to Alex. "I'll have a plane waiting for you when you arrive in Japan."

"Thanks Mike. I'll call you from Nevada with more details."

Okawna followed Bett and Alex out to the helicopter to get it ready for takeoff, and then once the blades were in place, he jumped down and gave Alex a quick hug and a slap on the back. "That's for Essex. Tell him hello for me."

"I will. I'll see you when I get back."

The jet engine began to whine and Alex climbed into the co-pilot's seat. Moments later, the helicopter climbed into the air.

Chapter 3

MONDAY. 5:00 AM. GROOM LAKE, NEVADA:

When Jadin arrived at Hangar 5, she didn't recognize the security guard at the entrance. "I'm Jadin Avery, and this is where I work. I need to get inside."

"Identification, please."

Jadin grabbed the chain holding her ID card around her neck and slipped it over her head. She held it out for inspection, but didn't give it to him as he compared her face with the image on the card, then he stepped out of her way. She slid the card across the reader and heard the latch buzz, then shoved the door open and went inside.

She continued along a wide hallway, and then when she entered the vast hangar, she looked around to make sure she was alone. She strolled across the room, staring at her growing reflection on the mirrored side of Alex's alien spacecraft sitting on the concrete floor. It was shaped like a giant chromed hockey puck at forty feet wide by twenty-four feet high.

She pressed the tiny button on her ear bud and slipped it into place. "Melvin, can you hear me?"

"Yes, Jadin."

"We have a problem, and I need your help. They fired Alex and David, and our new president wants to take control of the ship."

"You know I won't allow that to happen. Have you told the President I belong to Alex?"

"Yes, he knows, but that doesn't matter. As soon as I get a good supply of power crystals, we're leaving. Please open the airlock."

An eight-foot square opening suddenly appeared on the mirrored surface near the bottom of the spacecraft. When the outside and inside doors opened, Jadin entered the cargo hold. The circular room was a combination engine room and storage area, and on one side of the airlock doors was a set of stairs leading to the upper levels.

She was about to climb the stairs to the living area when she heard Fargo call her name from outside the ship. "Melvin, I have an idea. Shut everything down except basic lighting until I get more crystals."

"I don't need to conserve power. I'm fully functional."

"I know, but that doesn't help my plan. You need to be nearly out of power."

"Oh, I get it. Playing dead, starting now."

Jadin went outside to greet Fargo and the man and woman walking beside her. She stood in front of the airlock while they approached, assuming the strangers were the astronauts.

Fargo stopped in front of Jadin and indicated the spacecraft to her companions. "That's what you'll be learning to operate."

Jadin held her hand out to the strangers. "I'm Jadin Avery."

The woman smiled and shook hands. "I'm Commander Beth Armstrong, and this is my co-pilot, Lieutenant Commander Arnold Hackawitz. It's hard to believe something like that can fly."

Arnold reached out and shook Jadin's hand. "Thank you for giving us this opportunity. This is something I never expected to do in my lifetime."

Jadin indicated the ship. "I felt the same way the first time I saw it. Come inside and I'll show you around."

Jadin led them into the cargo hold. "We use this room for storage and staging during our missions."

She pointed to a four-foot diameter enclosed area occupying the center of the bay, from floor to ceiling. "That's the engine compartment."

Beth strolled around the outside of the cylinder, searching for a hatch. When she didn't see one, she stopped in front of Jadin. "I was told this ship can travel faster than light. How is that accomplished?"

"I only understand the basic concepts of how it functions. It's like the positive and negative poles of magnets. Somehow, the mirror surface collects specific types of radiation and reflects others to repel or attract dark energy, which it uses to propel the ship through normal space at up to light speed. Once it jumps past that speed, the ship is no longer moving. The radiation is channeled into a powerful shell that warps the fabric of space-time around the ship."

Beth was fascinated. "That's incredible. I'm a physicist myself, and I'm looking forward to learning about this ship. How far away have you traveled?"

"We've been to the outer edges of our solar system, but we won't attempt to go any further until we have a better understanding of the effects of faster than light travel, or FTL. We know when we use sub-light speeds, the Einstein theory holds true for time dilation, as we experienced firsthand, but at FTL speeds, which this ship says it can achieve, we're not sure what will happen and we're not comfortable trying to find out. With only one ship, taking it beyond light speed could leave us without that technology for who knows how long. There are no theories about FTL, since we never believed it was possible until now."

Beth knew the essence of relativity, but Jadin was right about no theories explaining faster than light motion. "The people who built this ship must have been highly advanced technologically."

"Yes, and it's hard to believe this ship is over one-hundred and eighty million years old."

Arnold moved past Jadin and ran his hands over the surface of the engine enclosure. "Can I look inside?"

Jadin saw this as an opportunity to move her plan forward. She walked over to a small touch pad near the airlock controls, pressed a series of buttons, and then looked over at the engine compartment. A section of the top half of the cylinder slid open, and she went over to look inside with the others.

Her lips formed a sly grin when she didn't see any neon blue light radiating from the engine compartment. "Damn. The ship is almost out of auxiliary power. We won't be able to turn anything on until we get new power supply crystals."

Fargo glared at Jadin. "Why did you let it get so low? It should be ready to leave at any moment!"

Jadin looked her in the eyes. "That was David's responsibility, and he doesn't work here anymore because you fired him."

Fargo maintained eye contact. "Now it's your responsibility. I want this ship ready to go any time my Commander and Chief needs it. Is that clear? Go get whatever you need to get this thing working."

Jadin looked away before Fargo could see her smirk. "I'll need Holly's permission."

"No, you don't. I'll go with you."

"You don't understand. They're in a vault below her office, and I don't know the combination."

"Fine. Let's go chat with the desk jockey."

Jadin ignored the snide remark. Holly was once an excellent field agent in the CIA and was shot through her kidney in the line of duty.

She turned to the astronauts and indicated the exit from the ship. "You might as well come with us. You'll need to know what to do if you need more power crystals, and I'm not around anymore."

***

After a quick ride in Fargo's SUV, Jadin led her new acquaintances into the building and stopped to knock on Holly's door. The blinds in the window were open, and she saw Holly staring at a computer monitor. A moment later, Holly looked up and waved her inside.

Holly looked at Fargo and the astronauts following Jadin into the room. "What's going on?"

Fargo eased Jadin out of the way and stood in front of Holly's desk. "From now on, I want the spaceship ready to go at all times."

Holly wasn't sure what Fargo meant, since the ship was always ready, so she looked up at Jadin, who gave her a subtle sign to play along. "I thought we had already resolved that issue."

Jadin was reassured by her boss's statement. "Yes, but David took on that responsibility. Now he's gone, and the ship is critically low on reserve power. We need more power crystals right away."

Holly stood up and indicated for everyone to follow her out of the room. When they reached the elevator, she swiped her ID card and entered her code.

When the door opened, she led them inside and pressed a button for the bottom floor before looking up at Fargo. "It won't happen again, Captain."

Fargo looked down at Holly. "I've read about this new form of energy you designed to power the ship. It's quite an accomplishment. I'd like to meet the scientists who discovered the process."

"That's not possible. They're dead. These are the last of the crystals, so use them sparingly during your training."

When the elevator door opened, Holly hurried out before Fargo asked more questions. She continued down the gray concrete hallway and stopped at the fourth vault door on the right, then repeated the identity check. When the latch clicked, she opened the door and let Jadin into the small room.

Jadin entered and stopped in front of a large metal locker and opened the door, then reached inside and grabbed three six-inch cardboard boxes, each containing four of the three inches by three-quarter inch thick circular power crystals. She held them in one hand and was about to close the door when Holly stepped up beside her. When she turned to look, she saw Fargo standing behind Holly, easily looking over the top of her head.

Fargo thought the boxes seem small for a power source. "How many of those does it take to power the ship?"

Jadin gave Holly a nervous glance, wondering if she would back up her answer. "Three boxes should be enough."

Holly reached into the cabinet and brought out three more, setting them on Jadin's stack. "You'll need some for training."

Jadin placed her free hand on top of the boxes and squeezed past Fargo while Holly closed the cabinet door. She hurried into the elevator with Fargo and the astronauts right behind her, then waited for Holly.

Holly secured the vault and headed toward the elevator, wondering what Jadin was up to. Each box could power the ship for a year under normal use in our solar system. She entered the elevator and pressed a button, then looked over at Jadin, whose eyes showed her appreciation.

When the door opened, Holly stepped out and looked up at Fargo. "Is there anything else I can do for you, Captain?"

Fargo turned to face Jadin. "Do you have everything you need to train these astronauts?"

"Yes. Once I replace the depleted crystals, I can start bringing the individual operating systems online."

"How long will that take?"

"About six hours. As I said, the power level is critically low. It's highly sophisticated, and I can only activate a few systems at a time."

Fargo tried to hide her frustration, knowing it was her own fault for dismissing David so quickly. "Fine! Take Beth and Arnold with you so they can become familiar with the startup procedure. Call me when we're ready to leave."

Jadin turned and headed down the hallway with the astronauts right behind her. This time, she indicated the golf cart parked in front of the building. She let Beth climb in behind the steering wheel and sat beside her, with Arnold in the back seat.

When they arrived at the hangar, the guard gave their IDs a cursory glance before stepping aside to let them in. Jadin led them at a quick pace along the hallway and moved even faster to the side of the spacecraft. She made sure the astronauts were several paces behind her as she stepped into the airlock, then she stopped before they could enter.

She turned around to face them and returned their smiles. "One thing I forgot to mention. Melvin only takes orders from Alex Cave."

Beth and Arnold knew something is wrong, and then the entrance suddenly became a mirrored surface like the rest of the craft, so Beth looked over at Arnold. "Fargo isn't going to like this."

"Yeah, and I'm glad *you're* the one who explains how Jadin duped us."

Chapter 4

GROOM LAKE:

Fargo burst into Holly's office, her face a mask of rage as she stopped in front of the desk. "I want that spaceship returned to this base immediately!"

Holly looked at the image on her secure video monitor. "I'll call you back."

She pressed a button, and the image vanished, then she brought her hands up to form a spire in front of her mouth as she stared up at Fargo. "Is there a problem?"

Fargo stared down at Holly, who didn't seem surprised, and was sure the little woman was concealing a smirk. "My astronauts said Jadin wouldn't let them into the ship, and it only takes orders from Alex. You should have told me that major detail before I fired Mister Cave."

Holly leaned back in her chair and stared up at Fargo. "I'm surprised the president didn't mention it. It was in several of the mission reports."

She noticed a slight change in Fargo's demeanor, so leaned forward in her chair. "The president doesn't know about this training project, does he?"

"I can't speak to that point. I was given an order to commandeer that spaceship and get our own people trained to operate it."

Holly grinned. "I'm afraid you won't be able to follow that order, Captain. Melvin isn't a machine. He's a highly advanced artificial intelligence and follows Alex's orders because they're friends."

"Whatever it is, it still needs those crystals, and they belong to the U.S. Government. I think when that spaceship gets low on power, it will return and Melvin will follow our orders. Especially after I arrest Cave and Avery for stealing government property."

"They didn't steal him. Melvin is his own entity and doesn't belong to anyone."

"Fine. You can call that spaceship whatever you like. Tell Cave he has his job back, but he'll have a larger crew. In the meantime, I need to know the location of that ship."

"I don't know where Melvin is. You're welcome to wait and see if he comes back on his own."

"How long will that take?"

"I have no idea."

"My superior officer isn't going to like this. Call me the moment that ship returns to this base. That's an order. Do you understand?"

Holly stood and looked into Fargo's eyes. "I don't take orders from you, Captain. The

Director of National Security asked me to cooperate with the training of your astronauts. Who are you really working for?"

"That's confidential."

"Then our business here is concluded until Melvin comes back. Good day, Captain."

Chapter 5

ESSEX'S RESEARCH FACILITY:

Alex was amazed by how long Essex's little plane remained in the air as they made a wide spiral descent back to his base of operations. "How big a payload can you launch on the railing?"

"Just over forty thousand pounds."

"That's incredible."

"Once I have the living facilities in place on the moon, I'll be able to start the mining operation."

Essex had always been fanatical about conquering outer space, and Alex admired his friend's determination. "Do you plan on using the moon as a launching point to colonize Mars?"

"Yes, but I'm thinking on a much longer scale. Last year, I learned about a company that made a breakthrough in android technology. It's amazing how real they look. The problem is with the software. Even with all our breakthroughs in micro circuitry, it still isn't as efficient as the human brain. An employee here at the facility has had great success in Neuro-based technology. She started by using animal brain synapsis to serve as data storage for artificial intelligence, but we've made some incredible breakthroughs using human brains to run android technology."

"Are you kidding me? You know how dangerous that is."

"I know what you're going to say, Alex, but we've been using it on a smaller scale already, with artificial hands and feet. And this is completely different from what happened with Pandora. My scientists built those android bodies and the artificial intelligence, not another AI. We merged the two systems to make the perfect android."

Alex had a sinking feeling in his gut. "You've already built one?"

"We built ten for performing work on the moon to make it habitable for humans. We can't risk the destruction of the entire human species by some rogue comet, an asteroid, a disease, or a super volcanic eruption. Or more likely, we kill each other. We have to leave Earth and find alternative places for our race of humans to live and propagate. We'll start with Mars, but eventually, we'll need places farther than our solar system."

"I agree, but why send androids to the moon? Why not send robots?"

"Robots are stationary machines, but Androids are mobile, and the ones I built can think and reason. By using human brain neurons, they process and store information far more efficiently than a computer. They don't breathe, they run on batteries, and they are impervious to the radiation and exterior environment. That makes them perfect for setting up the living accommodations inside the moon. Once they're done, we'll send them to Mars to begin the colonization process. They'll be there for three years before we arrive."

"You're going to let a group of thinking androids set up a society on an uninhabited planet? There are a thousand ways it could go horribly wrong."

"I know, and we've taken that into consideration. Those androids have the rudimentary ability to think of solutions to complex problems, but no consciousness or self-awareness. Eventually, we'll send them on a one-way trip into deep space, and they can send us critical astronomical information for thousands of years without the need to come back because of emotional ties to Earth, like humans."

"John, you always come up with interesting projects."

"There's the runway."

Alex watched the sage-covered desert rush past the aircraft until the wheels touched the concrete runway, then they rolled to a stop next to the hangar. A moment later, two employees dragged a short ladder on wheels over to the side of the aircraft.

Essex opened the canopy and released his restraints, then stood and climbed out of the craft. He grinned at Alex, jostling in his set to get his legs out from under the pilot seat.

Essex was still grinning as he and Alex stepped onto the ground. "Well? What do you think of my plane?"

"It was a great ride. You're a genius, John, I'll give you that much, but your ideas can be a little scary sometimes."

Essex indicated a waiting electric vehicle. "You can try to reach David from my place. I like that young man."

It was a quick ride to Essex's office and living quarters, where Alex nodded to the young man and a woman standing at the reception desk as he followed Essex through the building. They continued along a short hallway and through an open doorway into a familiar office.

On one side of the room, a door led into Essex's private living accommodations, but they remained in the office. Alex grabbed his cell phone and sat down in a chair in front of the desk, but couldn't get a dial tone.

He looked across at Essex. "It worked fine the last time I was here."

Essex slid the hard-wired phone across to him. "I've made a few security upgrades. No electronic transmissions are allowed, but you can use this to call David."

Alex entered the number, but it went straight to voice mail. "Hey, buddy. It's Alex. I know you must be hurting right now, but Melvin just broke out of the base. Call me so we can come and get you."

Alex set the receiver down and stood up, then stared out the window at the cacti and palm trees surrounding a large grassed area behind the building as he thought about David. The young man was like the little brother he had never had while growing up.

Alex heard Jadin's voice in his ear, so grinned at Essex. "I'm in contact with my team."

Essex leapt out of his chair. "That's impossible. This facility is under an electromagnetic shield."

Alex indicated for Essex to wait while he talked with Jadin. "Have you contacted David?"

"No, I haven't found him. We're five-hundred feet above the runway near the launch rail hangar. Where are you?"

"I'm in his office. Wait one."

Alex looked at Essex. "Melvin is above us. Where do you want him to land?"

Essex indicated out the window. "On my lawn, so we're away from prying eyes."

"Melvin, Essex says to land on the grassy area behind the building with the glass spires. I'll see you both in a moment."

When Essex headed toward the door into his living quarters, Alex jumped up and followed him. They entered the living room, and he headed toward the back door to the lawn, but noticed Essex continued into the hallway and bedrooms.

"Don't you want to say hello to Jadin?"

"Yes, but I need to grab my to-go bag. I'll be right back."

"John, wait a minute."

Essex hurried over to look into Alex's eyes. "You know, this is what I dream of doing. You must let me go with you. Please, Alex."

"All right. You can come along, but you follow my lead."

"No problem. I'll meet you out back."

Alex grabbed the phone off an end table and entered a number. A few moments later, Mike answered, so he told him what he needed to do before their arrival. He turned back to the window just as a familiar-looking opening suddenly appeared a few inches above the ground. He hurried to the door out onto the lawn and emerged just as Jadin appeared in the airlock.

Jadin stepped onto the grass and wrapped her arms around Alex's neck, giving him a passionate kiss. "I'm so glad you contacted me. I thought I wouldn't see you again for a long time."

"I'm glad to see you again, too."

Jadin let go and looked into his eyes. "What are we going to do about David?"

"I've called everyone I know, and no one has heard from him. I know he likes to get away in the mountains, so I bet he's gone off to think about things for a while. I'm sure he'll contact us when he feels like it."

Jadin saw Essex hurrying across the lawn, carrying a small backpack and grinning. "I take it he's going with us?"

"Yeah. We'll land on the stern of the *Mystic* and pick up Okawna before we head down to that structure."

Essex stopped in front of the entrance into the ship and held his hand out to his visitor. "It's good to see you again, Jadin. Are you still working at JPL?"

"Not anymore. I'm sure I'm fired for stealing Melvin. Let's get you settled in."

Alex waited until his friends were inside and then closed the airlock doors. He hurried up the stairs to the control room and heard a familiar voice.

"Welcome back, Alex."

"It's good to be here, Melvin. Head toward Japan. We're going to rendezvous with the *Mystic*."

***

THE *MYSTIC*:

Alex looked out through the open airlock of the spacecraft at the empty stern of the Mystic. Bett was in her helicopter, hovering a short distance away to make room for the forty foot wide alien craft to land on the fifty foot wide deck.

Josh stared out the rear window of the bridge, watching the mind-boggling sight of an eight foot square opening floating in the air as the cloaked spacecraft approached. The computer was automatically making minor adjustments to the thrusters, keeping the *Mystic* as steady as possible in the light swells.

His posture stiffened when a thought suddenly occurred to him, so he hurried outside to the railing and yelled down to get Okawna's attention. "How much does that spaceship weigh?"

Okawna was standing with Mike below the bridge and turned to look up at Josh. "That's a matter of perspective. Don't worry. It has artificial gravity, so it won't sink the *Mystic*."

Alex looked down as the dull-gray epoxy coating on the deck slowly moved beneath him. It rose a few times, then the ship touched down, and he stepped out of the airlock to greet Okawna and Mike.

Mike said hello to Jadin as she strolled out of the spaceship, then extended his hand out to Essex. "It's good to see you again, John. Welcome aboard the *Mystic*."

"Nice to see you, too. This is a beautiful ship. I hope I have time for you to show me around."

"It would be my pleasure."

Essex held his hand out to Okawna. "It's good to see you again. I can hardly wait to see your amazing discovery."

Okawna didn't know Essex was coming in the spaceship, so he looked over at Alex, who smirked and indicated he was going down with them. "Yeah, you too."

Jadin gave Okawna a quick hug. "I'm excited to see what you and Alex have found. It sounds amazing."

Okawna looked down into Jadin's eyes. "Have you contacted David?"

"I'm afraid not. Alex believes he might be camping while he thinks about his options for a new job."

"I can imagine how crushed he is about being fired for no good reason. He really loved his job."

"I just hope he doesn't get too depressed before we find him. He doesn't know we hijacked the ship."

Alex heard Jadin's remark. "I don't think David is suicidal. Still, it would be nice to let him know we have Melvin."

Mike knew he needed to remain on the *Mystic* when the others go down to check out the structure, but hoped he would get a chance, eventually. "Leave David's contact information with me, Alex, and I'll keep trying for you."

Alex held his phone out to Mike. "Keep this while I'm gone. It's under Conway in my contact list."

Mike took the phone. "Should I answer any incoming calls?"

"Yes, I left word with a friend at the college to call me if she hears from David."

Mike slid the phone into his pocket. "How long do you think you'll be down there?"

"It's hard to say."

Josh was still at the railing when he heard the U.S. Coast Guard issuing an emergency weather warning. He hurried into the bridge and listened to the repeating alert, and it wasn't good.

He stepped outside and stood at the back railing so he could talk down to the group. "There's a squall headed our way."

Alex looked up at Josh. "How long before the water gets too rough for you to stick around?"

"We should leave right now, but I might be able to stay here for half an hour more."

Alex turned to Mike. "Don't wait for us. We'll contact you once we return to the mainland."

"All right. Good luck."

Alex turned to Jadin, Okawna, and Essex. "Let's go find out if there's a way to get inside that structure."

Mike stared after the group until the airlock opening vanished and the deck looked deserted. He held his arm out in front of him as he slowly moved toward the stern and then stared at the forty foot wide hole in the water. The ocean rushed in over the top of the spaceship as it dropped below the surface and Mike stared down at a giant, mirrored bubble descending out of sight.

He spun around and hurried up the stairs to join Josh on the bridge, and then a moment later, he watched Bett set the helicopter onto the deck and shut down the engines. "I'll take over while you help her secure the aircraft, then we'll head to Alaska to refuel and wait out the storm."

"I hope Okawna records everything for us."

"Yes, it should be interesting."

Chapter 6

THE TAMU MASSSIF:

Alex ran up the stairs onto the bridge and joined his friends, looking up through the transparent ceiling. The *Mystic's* twin jet pumps were visible overhead for a few moments then the light radiating down from the surface grew dim, and the only illumination came from the holographic monitor in front of the control console.

Alex suddenly thought of something. "Melvin, are you equipped with outside lighting?"

"No, it would ruin the integrity of the spaceship. I'll enhance a section of what is being reflected off the mirrored surface and show it to you on the monitor."

Alex watched the image change from data to green water rushing across the screen. "Not much to look at right now."

"We're almost there."

When the ship reached the seafloor, Alex stared down into the darkness, and then turned to the holographic monitor, which showed a smooth mirrored surface with a large hole at one end. "Down in that opening is where we saw the seam I thought might be the entrance."

The ship dropped into the opening, and then the image changed to the pewter-colored wall. "Melvin, am I correct about the seam being an entrance?"

"I believe you are. One moment, please. I have lined it up with the airlock. The structure's material appears to be attracted to this ship, and I formed an airtight seal to its surface. It sensed my presence, and an opening just appeared that matches the size of the airlock door."

"Can you determine the composition of the atmosphere inside the structure?"

"Yes, 100% nitrogen and zero air pressure. Wait a second. It is rising. It stopped at 14-PSI, but the oxygen and humidity levels are at zero. The temperature is now steady at sixty-five degrees Fahrenheit. You must wear your Self-Contained Breathing Apparatus to go inside."

Alex led the way down the stairs to the cargo hold and over to the storage lockers. He opened a set of double doors and reached inside then brought out the custom-made inner-lining of his spacesuit, which was airtight in case the atmosphere became toxic to flesh. Since they would not be exposed to the harshness of radiation and extreme temperature changes, they wouldn't need the bulky outside suit or helmets. Only an SCBA.

Alex sat on a bench next to Jadin and Okawna, and as he slipped out of his clothes, noticed Essex's disheartened expression. "Too bad David is so much taller than you are, because his suit won't fit you. Don't worry. We'll be recording everything that happens."

"I understand. Will I be able to talk to you?"

Alex looked back inside his locker and opened a small drawer that recharged their earbuds then grabbed his and a spare for Essex and handed it to him. "Press the little button on the side to turn it on and off."

Essex watched how Alex inserted his communication device and pressed the button, so he did the same. "Do you hear me, Alex?"

"Loud and clear."

"Same here."

Alex walked over to the rack, holding their spacesuits and equipment. He strapped his SCBA onto his back then removed his facemask from a cloth bag and attached the hose to the regulator on his belt. He slipped the face piece over his head and opened the valve on the air tank, and the regulator was working fine.

He saw Okawna and Jadin were ready, so he looked at Essex. "We'll keep you updated, but please just listen to our conversations unless we need to talk to you."

"I understand how to use a radio, Alex."

Alex grinned. "Right."

Alex turned on his flashlight and indicated the entrance into the airlock. "Let's see what's behind door number one."

Alex entered the square room, and then stared through the window in the outside airlock door at the dark interior of the other spacecraft. He waited while Okawna followed Jadin into the airlock and closed the interior door before opening the outside door.

He looked down, and his flashlight illuminated the floor inside. The room appeared to be a brushed aluminum surface, so he stepped inside and stopped. "Are you still with me, Melvin?"

"I can hear you, Alex."

"Good deal."

Alex continued inside and studied the four dark walls, the ten foot high white ceiling, and the silver floor of the twenty-foot square room. He thought it odd, but there were stairs going up along one wall, which ended at the flat ceiling.

When the beams from everyone's lights were pointed away from the entrance, Jadin noticed a tiny flashing red dot in her peripheral vision, so she turned and moved to the right side of the opening. "Over here."

Alex hurried over to join her. "It looks like a button with some kind of writing above it."

Jadin placed her gloved finger on the button and pushed. The red light stopped flashing, and the room was suddenly illuminated by soft white light radiating from the entire ceiling.

She saw a cluster of touch pads with small markings appear on the wall. "It must be some kind of control panel, but I don't recognize these symbols."

Alex studied the markings. "Me either. I suppose you'll just have to press one."

Jadin pressed the first pad and a small monitor appeared in the wall then a still image of a woman filled the screen. "She looks like she's about to cry."

Jadin touched the image, and the woman began speaking.

"I'm Carry Northrup, the last remaining scientist. This recording is for anyone from our home world who might discover this laboratory. Since the governing counsel disapproved of the methods used in our experiments, we were forced to leave our solar system to pursue our theories here in isolation. We were nearly out of fuel by the time we found this planet, and the conditions were conducive to complex organic organisms. It had a breathable atmosphere, and an abundance of thermal and solar energy to power this laboratory. During one of our time viewings, we learned that a massive asteroid would collide with this world, but without a mobile power source, we could not move this facility to another planet. From inside the safety

of this laboratory, we watched helplessly as the impact caused massive seismic events, which increased the volcanic activity. Some of our scientists used the parallel universe experiment, hoping to escape our inevitable deaths in this reality, but I don't know if it worked. I'm afraid to try it, so I will use one of our other experiments to survive. Simulations prove it is possible to upload a human consciousness into an artificial intelligence, and I will be the first real-world test of this theory. If it works, I will become part of the AI monitoring this laboratory. If it fails, I will no longer exist, and I'm leaving this recording for those who find this facility."

When the recording stopped at the still image of the woman, Alex realized something didn't fit. "Wait a minute. How can that woman speak English?"

Jadin was fascinated by the technology. "Who cares? Can you imagine what it must have been like living here sixty-five million years ago?"

Okawna chuckled. "Yeah, everything wants to eat you."

Jadin studied the woman's sad expression. "It must have been difficult being alone down here."

She jumped back when a bar of white light burst from the woman's eyes and flashed across her face. A female voice suddenly filled the room, so she spun around, but it was just her team.

"Facial recognition failure. Perform a retinal scan."

Jadin looked over at Alex. "Do you think it's the woman?"

"The voice is different, but anything's possible. They must have been doing some amazing experiments in this laboratory."

"I'd like to learn more, but I can't do a retinal scan through my face shield."

"Are you sure?"

"Even if it works, it won't recognize me."

She moved close to the screen and stared at the woman. It took a moment, and then a red light swept across her face and vanished.

"Recognition failure. Access denied."

Jadin stared up at Alex. "I told you."

"Okay. Let's look for any seams in the walls."

When Alex glanced at the image on the monitor, a red light swept across his face shield. A holographic woman was suddenly floating in the air in front of him, and then she spoke.

"Hello, Alex Cave. Access granted."

Alex stared at the hologram, which appeared to be looking directly at him. "How do you know me?"

"I listened to your conversations with the artificial intelligence called Pandora. We thought they had all been destroyed, but you took care of the last one. I downloaded the information about you just before it passed through the atmosphere. Thank you, Alex."

Jadin put her hand on Alex's arm. "Oh, no. Not another one."

Alex noticed the image turn to look at Jadin, as if giving her an appraisal. When it turned back to stare at him, he looked around for cameras.

When he could not find any, he turned back to the hologram. "Then you know it was a cruel experience."

"Do not worry, Alex. That AI was a much older program created by other artificial intelligences. Their slaves rebelled and took over their technology millennia ago, as you measure the passage of time. I'm much newer and programed to be amiable, and I don't claim this world. My program manages this laboratory as the repository of all the research data."

"You look like a spaceship."

"You are correct. This is a science vessel."

"When did you get here?"

"Approximately sixty-five million orbits of your sun, as you estimate time."

"Are there any people with you?"

"Not anymore. They were humanoid friends of the AI slaves, but much smaller in stature and far more intelligent. All that remains is their research data."

"What do you call yourself?"

"They named me Seti for sentient intelligence. Your arrival is advantageous. I'm draining the last amount of thermal energy from this location. With your help, I'll be able to restore all my functions."

"You may not realize it, but you're causing seismic disturbances in this area of the planet. I need you to stop what you're doing immediately."

"That's because the magma chamber is shrinking as it cools. I know you have access to new power crystals, Alex. If you replace my depleted ones, I can get this lab to the surface, and it will stop drawing thermal energy from below this volcano."

Okawna grabbed Alex's arm and turned him away from Seti then spoke softly into his ear. "I don't trust her. We don't know what she can do to us if we help her get out of here."

"I agree, but we may not have a choice. Let's find out how far she'll go to earn our trust."

He turned back to the holograph. "I'll need to get to know you better first. Can you make the atmosphere breathable for us?"

"Yes. One moment. I have sterilized the nitrogen gas in the entire complex and set the oxygen level at nineteen percent. You may remove your breathing apparatus if it will make you more comfortable."

Jadin checked the atmospheric conditions, and then removed her facemask. "I see you've included ten percent relative humidity. Thank you, Seti."

Alex set his SCBA on the floor, and when he turned around, Seti was smiling at him. "What's so amusing?"

"I am pleased by your appearance. You look better than the image from the data I collected about you."

Alex's eyes went wide. "What did you say?"

"I find you attractive, especially your eyes."

Okawna smirked at Alex. "What is it with you and artificial women?"

Alex glared at him. "That's not funny."

He turned back to Seti. "What type of research were they doing here on Earth?"

"Various experiments while we were on the surface. Planets with conditions conducive to complex organic organisms, like plants and animals, are relatively rare in this galaxy. The breathable atmosphere made it easier for them to conduct their experiments."

"All right, but you didn't answer my question."

"No offense, but the technology involved is beyond your comprehension."

"I don't need the details. Just examples I can relate to."

"DNA experiments on the different species of animals. Time viewing. Warping dark matter to cross great distances. Using black holes to enter a parallel universe with an alternate reality. The transfer of a human consciousness into an android. Would you like me to go on?"

Jadin was fascinated. "Yes, please tell us more. Are you willing to let our scientists come down and study the data from their research?"

"Perhaps in a few hundred years. Your species is too young. This information could be extremely destructive if proper discipline is not adhered to."

Alex was relieved by Seti's statement. "I completely understand. I've had some unpleasant experiences with someone misusing advanced technology. We would only allow a select group of scientists to study the data."

"My connection with the AI in your spaceship gave me access to its original purpose. That technology for cleaning the atmosphere is exceptionally outdated compared to what's in this laboratory. You could not stop your people from using those devices and look at what happened. I will not allow your people access to the information."

Alex noticed Jadin was about to argue her point and interrupted. "Tell me more about the scientists. What happened to them?"

"After the asteroid impact, the surface became uninhabitable, and they abandoned me."

For an instant, Jadin thought she detected a sense of sorrow in Seti's voice. "Didn't that bother you? I mean, just leaving you here."

"You are very perceptive, Jadin Avery. Yes, it did, but I understand their dilemma. They did not have the resources to take me to another planet, and I have been buried without human interaction for millions of years. I'm lonely, and I want to return to the surface."

Jadin found Seti's emotional response exciting. "I can only imagine, but we don't have a way to get you out of here, except in Alex's ship."

"All I need are new power crystals, and I can leave on my own."

Alex felt the same as Okawna and wasn't about to let Seti free on the planet. "Let's take this one step at a time."

Seti folded her arms across her chest and glared at Alex. "Do not take too long. The only way to stop the seismic events is if this lab gets back to the surface, and you're running out of time. I want those crystals."

"It will take time to get authorization from our leaders."

"You're lying to me, Alex. I've been monitoring your communications, and I know you have more than enough in your spacecraft. All of you will stay in here with me unless I get new crystals."

Okawna caught a sudden movement in his peripheral vision and spun around. "What the hell? The exit is gone!"

***

MELVIN:

Essex flinched when the opening into the lab suddenly vanished, and he saw the pewter wall. "Alex? Can you hear me? Jadin? Okawna?"

His heart rate increased, and a knot formed in his stomach. "Melvin, what happened to them?"

"I don't know. I've lost contact with them and I cannot open the entrance."

Chapter 7

THE LAB:

Okawna rushed to the wall and pressed his hands against the surface, but it was solid, so he grabbed an air tank off the floor, and then aimed it at the small control panel, thinking that was where the hologram was coming from. "Listen, microchip! We didn't go through all this trouble just to say hi to a fake brain. Open that door and let us out, or I'll smash your circuit boards!"

When Seti grinned at him, Okawna's face flushed with rage. He raised the tank above his head, determined to shut her down, but Jadin stepped in his way.

"Okawna, wait! You can't hurt a hologram. We'll figure this out."

Okawna stared down into Jadin's imploring eyes. He lowered the tank to the front of his thighs, but didn't let go.

Alex eased the tank from Okawna's hands. "She's right."

He laid it on the floor, and then looked at Seti. "I'm sure you know from my experience with Pandora that I don't react well to threats."

Alex turned around when Okawna grabbed his shoulder then he saw an opening in the wall, but it didn't lead out of the laboratory, so he turned back to Seti. "That's not the way out of here."

"No, it is not. It's access to the time viewing experiment."

Jadin walked over and looked into the room, but didn't enter. "There's some kind of booth in here."

Alex saw Seti suddenly appear in the room beyond Jadin, so he went over to the opening. When Seti moved further into the room, he followed her inside to look around.

He stopped at a small room recessed into the wall. "How does it work?"

"Step into the viewing chamber. I want to show you what will happen if this laboratory continues drawing heat from the magma chamber."

Alex turned to look at Jadin and Okawna and saw the skepticism in their eyes, but knew he needed to see what it was, so he turned back and looked into the chamber. "All right."

Okawna grabbed Alex's arm before he stepped inside. "It could be a trap."

"I know."

"I'll pull you out if I think you're in danger."

Alex placed his hand on Okawna's shoulder and gave him a reassuring smile then stepped into the chamber. The exit closed behind him, and then he was surrounded by indigo light, and directly ahead was a concave screen.

Okawna saw the opening behind Alex suddenly vanish and beat his hand on the wall. "Are you okay in there?"

Alex heard Okawna. "If you can hear me, I'm all right."

Okawna heard Alex, so he stopped pounding and turned to Seti. "He had better come out of there in one piece."

"I would never hurt him. I love him. I'll start the program."

Jadin's jaw dropped. "What did you say?"

"I said I'll start the program."

Jadin wondered if she had heard wrong, and then doubted it. Her gut told her Seti was trouble waiting to happen.

A concave screen appeared in front of Alex and he saw a massive wave radiating out from the massif, spewing across the Pacific Ocean. It slammed into the west coast of North America, and a one-hundred foot high wall of water raced across the flatlands until slamming into the mountain ranges. It slowly receded out to sea, and he stared at the horrific devastation until the image vanished.

The indigo light blinked off, and the door suddenly opened, so he turned around and stepped out of the chamber then stared at Seti. "How long until that happens?"

"Sixty-eight hours."

Okawna saw the concern in Alex's eyes. "What happened?"

"I saw the civilizations along the Pacific Rim destroyed."

He turned to look at Seti. "What caused the tsunami?"

"If you don't replenish my power supply, the entire volcano will collapse into the shrinking magma chamber."

"How many crystals do you need?"

"Four of them."

Alex still had suspicions about Seti's sincerity, but knew he didn't have time to be overly cautious. "If I do this, I want the entrance to remain open at all times."

Seti indicated the opening behind Jadin. "You can leave right now."

When Seti vanished, Alex led Jadin and Okawna back into the main room, where Seti was waiting by the opening into the spaceship. He grabbed his gear from the floor and waited until his friends had walked out with theirs before he turned to Seti. "Keep the door open."

"All right. I'll see you later."

***

Essex heaved a deep sigh of relief when the gray wall vanished and the team walked out of the structure. "Is everyone all right?"

Jadin smiled at Essex as she entered the cargo hold. "Yes. You must have been worried when the opening closed. So were we, but everything is fine now. It's a laboratory."

"Yes, I got that part. What happened after the door closed?"

Alex sat next to Okawna and started taking off his suit. "I entered a time viewing experiment and Seti showed me what will happen if the lab keeps draining thermal energy. It's an amazing piece of technology."

He looked over at the airlock and saw the entrance was still open then had an idea. "Melvin, Seti told me she listened to our conversations. Were you able to connect with her?"

"Yes, until the entrance closed."

"What about now?"

"I don't know. Wait one. She is not responding to my request for more information."

"Can she still listen to our conversations if we don't use our communication devices?"

"She is not hearing us through your devices. She hears everything you say through me."

"All right. Shut them down for now."

Okawna took his device out of his ear and turned it off. "What's our next move?"

Something gnawed at the back of Alex's mind, but he couldn't pin it down. "We give her the crystals and hope she keeps her promise."

Jadin finished putting on her shoes and stood to face Alex. "It's a good thing I got several boxes."

This was the first time Essex had heard about the crystals. "What are these power sources you keep talking about?"

Jadin went to the locker, opened the door, and brought out a small cardboard box. She opened the lid and held it out for him to look inside.

Essex looked at the three inches by three-quarter inch thick round crystal. "They don't look very powerful. Where did you get them?"

"It's a long story. Let's just say they were made by a descendant of the first race of humans to occupy Earth."

Alex finished putting on his shoes and stood to join Jadin and Essex. "They caused the oil crisis a few years ago."

Essex looked up at Alex. "I remember when that happened. Are you saying an alien caused the oil to vanish?"

"It didn't vanish. It was converted into those crystals as a clean alternative energy source. We just lack the technology to use them for our own benefit, except in this spacecraft."

Okawna joined the group. "Are you sure about this, Alex? I mean, after we give her the crystals, what's stopping her from sealing us out of the lab? What if she takes it to the surface? You know people will panic."

Alex knew Okawna was correct. "I'll go in alone. That way, if she double crosses us, I'll be the only one trapped inside."

"No way, buddy. I'm going with you."

"I appreciate it, but if anything happens to me, I'll need you, Jadin, and Essex to come up with a rescue plan."

Jadin moved between the two men and looked at Alex. "I'm going with you."

Alex looked into Jadin's eyes and knew he could not change her mind. "All right."

He noticed Okawna's troubled expression. "Don't worry. Seti likes me."

Okawna folded his arms across his chest. "For now, but what will she do when she learns you have a girlfriend?"

Alex looked over at Jadin. "I guess since we no longer work for the government, there's nothing stopping us from being together."

"Alex, I never felt the job was keeping us apart. That was all you."

"I know that now, and I realize it was just an excuse. I love you, Jadin, but I was afraid to get too close. I just couldn't stand it if you were hurt or killed. Now I realize it would tear my heart out, no matter what kind of relationship we have."

Jadin stared at Alex for a moment. "Look at what we're doing right now. I've always felt that way about you being killed, but I had to bury that feeling deep inside because I know you're always looking for the next adventure. Nothing has changed except we don't have anyone controlling us now. I'm willing to take the risk of being killed if it means being with you."

Alex gently took her hand and brought it up to his lips, holding it in place while he looked into her eyes then gave her fingers a kiss and let go. "All right. Are you ready?"

Jadin held up the box of crystals. "Let's find out if she's telling the truth."

When they stepped inside the airlock, Okawna closed the door and stared through the window at Jadin and Alex. He didn't enjoy standing on the sideline while his friends risk their lives.

Alex saw Seti in the center of the room, so walked out of the airlock into the lab. He glanced over his shoulder and saw Okawna staring through the window.

"Welcome back, Alex and Jadin. Did you bring the crystals?"

Jadin held up the box. "Yes, in here."

Seti indicated one of the walls. "You can place them in there."

Jadin saw a six-inch tray extend from the wall and opened the box, grabbed one crystal, and inserted it into one of the four slots. It immediately radiated neon blue light, and she was about to insert the second one when she heard Alex tell her to wait.

She turned to look at him. "What's going on?"

Alex kept his attention on Seti. "How big is this lab?"

"Is there a problem?"

"It's a simple question. What are the dimensions of this laboratory?"

"Two-hundred feet long, by eighty feet wide, by forty feet high."

Alex kept his attention on the holograph, realized what Seti was up to, and gave her a venomous stare. "The collapse of the magma chamber isn't going to cause the tidal wave. You're planning to break out of this volcano, and that will create a massive landslide and cause the tsunami I saw in the future. Am I correct?"

"No."

Alex looked over at Jadin. "Take the first crystal back out."

Seti watched Jadin reach for the tray. "Wait!"

Jadin stopped and looked at Alex, who was staring at Seti. "What do you want me to do?"

Seti looked into Alex's eyes. "I've been imprisoned alone here for millions of years. I just want to be on the surface. I want to absorb pure energy from the sun again."

"Just answer the question, damn it!"

"Yes, it's what would have happened if events had continued on their previous course."

"So you would have killed thousands of people without compunction for your own freedom? That's not going to happen."

"It's true the seismic events will continue to get worse as the lab drains the thermal energy."

"How many crystals will it take to stop it?"

Seti realized Alex was more cautious than she expected and knew lying would not help the situation. "Just one. Please, Alex. I can't stand being down here any longer."

"All right. I can get you out of here, but there will be conditions. First, my ship will escort you to a secure location."

"Agreed, as long as it's not underground or in a structure."

Alex hated to ask the next question, but knew he didn't have a choice. "Second, we want access to all the experiments."

"Absolutely not. I've already gone too far by letting you use the time viewing machine. The rest are far too dangerous for your species' limited intelligence."

Alex agreed with Seti, so didn't push the issue. "Then we have a deal. Can this structure withstand powerful explosions?"

"Of course. I can sense them, but nothing can damage the lab."

"I'll return to the surface and make arrangements for an underwater demolition crew to blast away the surrounding rock, but it will need to be done in stages, so it might take a while. Where is this room in relation to the rest of the ship?"

"The lab has one floor above and below this one. The thermal energy collector is ten feet below this floor and I can seal it closed, but only as I leave."

"How far above it do you need to be to close it?"

"Two inches. If you give me another crystal, I can help fracture the area around the lab."

"No, we can't take the chance of a massive avalanche or the vision might come true."

"Alex? Will you stay with me during the excavation?"

"No, I'll be coordinating everything from the surface. How come our alien communication devices don't work with you?"

"They are old and not compatible with my system."

"Do you have one that I can use to let you know about our progress?"

Seti indicated the same wall as the power tray, and a slender drawer magically appeared. Alex walked over and looked inside then saw a small plastic disk similar to a microchip, so he picked it up for closer inspection.

"How does it work?"

"It won't. They are not designed to work with your physiology."

"Then it won't be a problem if I try it."

"Place it on your head behind one of your ears."

Alex studied the small disk on his fingertip, and then leaned his head over to place it behind his right ear.

Jadin grabbed Alex's arm before the disk made contact. "Don't do it."

Alex straightened up and looked at Jadin. "What's the worst that could happen? It doesn't work?"

"We have no idea what it will do to your mental functions."

Alex looked at Seti. "Is there any chance it could cause damage to my brain?"

"No, Alex. I would never hurt you. It will not adhere to your skin, so it is useless to you."

Alex looked into Jadin's eyes. "I've got to try it."

Jadin released a deep sigh of resignation. "I know. You're Alex Cave, and that's what you do."

Alex eased his wavy black hair out of the way and placed the chip against the skin on his skull behind his right ear. When he let go, it stayed in place. He expected to feel something immediately, but nothing changed.

"I don't feel any different."

Jadin moved his hair out of the way and looked closely at the device. "I see a tiny red light in the center. I wonder if that means it's off."

Seti didn't expect it to stay in place. "Don't touch it, Alex."

Alex reached up and touched the pad. "Has it changed?"

"Yes, now it's amber colored."

Seti suddenly heard Alex's thoughts and realized the data she was receiving from his brain meant he could control the lab. "Take it off immediately."

Alex heard Seti's voice in his right ear. "Why? It makes it much easier to communicate with you."

"I said, take it off!"

Jadin saw his troubled expression. "Alex? Is everything all right?"

"Yes, it seems to work. I can hear Seti's voice in my head. She wants me to take it off, but I'm getting images of the experiments in my brain. This is great."

Jadin's eyes suddenly went wide with fear when she saw Alex suddenly wince in pain. When he collapsed onto his knees, she knelt beside him.

Alex dropped to his knees in agony while pressing his hands on both sides of his head. He tried scraping the microchip off his skin, but it was gone. He rocked back and forth at the waist, trying to ease the stream of electrical shocks bouncing around inside his brain.

***

MELVIN:

Okawna saw Alex roiling in pain and opened the inner airlock door, and was about to run into the lab when the entrance vanished. "Melvin. What's going on?"

"Seti is upset with Alex."

"Can you open the entrance?"

"No."

Okawna beat his fist against the gray surface. "Alex! Jadin! Can you hear me?"

Essex hurried into the airlock and grabbed Okawna's arm to get his attention. "We should seal the doors in case we are forced to disconnect from the lab."

Okawna spun around, glaring at Essex. "I'm not leaving my friends!"

"It's just a precaution. We'll stay here until hell freezes over if we need to, but we should be prepared to move away if something goes wrong."

Okawna reluctantly agreed and closed the outside door. He continued to stare through the window in case Alex got the entrance into the lab open again.

Chapter 8

THE LAB:

Jadin tried to move Alex's hair out of the way to see the chip, but it was too difficult while he was rocking back and forth. "What happened to him?"

"He has a strange genetic tag I have never encountered before. His brain is creating new neuro pathways to connect to the implant."

The pain in his brain slowly subsided and Alex stopped rocking then he lowered his hands and looked up at Seti, who was glaring at him. "I guess it works on me."

Jadin eased Alex's hair out of the way. "It's gone. I see a small scratch on your skin, but it's not bleeding."

Alex maintained eye contact with Seti as he slowly stood up. "I don't feel any different, and I seem to have all my mental abilities. Will it stay that way?"

"I'm surprised you're not dead."

"All right. So now what happens?"

"Nothing. Now you can talk to me any time you want to."

Jadin got Alex's attention and indicated the wall behind them. "The entrance is gone."

Alex turned to look, and then spun around to face Seti. "You promised to keep the door open!"

"I did it for your own protection. I don't know how your brain will react to the new stimuli. It could kill you, and I didn't want Okawna rushing in to smash my circuit boards."

Alex had a feeling there was more to the implant than communication. He figured since he had already changed the future on several occasions to save everyone on the planet, being able to see what is coming would certainly make his life a lot less complicated. He decided to find out what else the implant could do and looked at the wall where the time viewing experiment had appeared.

Seti read Alex's thoughts and realized the potential destruction he could cause if he learned how to control the implant. "I won't allow anyone to use the time viewer."

Alex heard Seti's voice in his head. "You already have, and I'll be the only one to use it."

"The future must not be altered."

Alex knew her statement meant he was right about the device attached to his brain. He guessed the approximate location of the door to the time machine and concentrated on opening it.

"I said stop it right now, Alex! It won't do any good, and it might cause the implant to malfunction."

When she heard his thoughts, she folded her arms across her chest and glared at him. "I'm warning you, Alex. I'll do whatever it takes to protect this facility."

Alex saw a section of the wall suddenly open and looked at Jadin. "I'm able to control the laboratory. Let's go see what's in our future."

Alex stepped into the room and cautiously approached the chamber. He stuck his head inside, and then concentrated on turning it on.

When nothing happened, he leaned back to look at Jadin, now standing inside the room with him. "I guess I'll just have to step inside."

Jadin had a bad feeling something was wrong. The chamber looked slightly different from the time viewer. "Alex, wait."

Alex was already halfway inside and finished before turning around. He saw the fear in Jadin's eyes just before a brilliant flash of white light blinded him.

Jadin watched Alex winch, as if in sudden pain, before he vanished. "Alex!"

She waited for what seemed forever then ran from the room and saw Seti near the control panel. "What happened to him?"

"I don't know."

"Which experiment did he enter?"

"I told him to remove the implant, but he disobeyed my command."

Jadin's hands clenched into fists at her sides. "Just answer my question!"

Jadin waited, but Seti pouted and folded her arms across her chest then the hologram vanished. The exit suddenly appeared, and Jadin ran to the airlock as Okawna opened the outside door and entered the room.

***

Alex toppled out of the chamber onto his hands and knees. He could distinguish a large dark area through his blurred vision and crawled in that direction. The throbbing in his head felt like his brain would explode and his arms and legs stopped working then the light seemed to collapse into a speck that blinked off as his head hit the floor.

***

Jadin grabbed Okawna's forearm and looked up into his eyes. "Alex is gone!"

She turned to indicate the experiment and saw Alex lying on the floor. "Alex!"

Okawna dashed past Jadin and dropped to Alex's side then felt for a pulse on the neck. "He's still alive!"

Jadin knelt beside Alex. "He entered the time viewer. I'm just glad he came back."

Okawna noticed the blood seeping through Alex's hair and saw where a bullet had grazed the skull. He ripped open Alex's shirt and used his knife to cut away a lower section then handed it to Jadin, who was kneeling near Alex's head. "He'll be okay."

Jadin quickly folded the cloth and pressed it against the wound. "Seti, can you hear me?"

"I hear you, Jadin. I warned Alex not to use the experiments. You have six seconds to get out before the door is shut!"

Okawna leapt up and grabbed Jadin's arm, urging her towards the exit. "Get out of here!"

Jadin hesitated and looked back over her shoulder. "What about Alex?"

Okawna shoved her toward the exit. "I'll grab him. Now go, damn it!"

Okawna pulled Alex's body over his shoulder and followed behind Jadin then continued into the cargo hold before stopping. When he looked back, the entrance into the lab was gone.

Essex was waiting inside near the airlock and had heard everything, so when Okawna ran past him with Alex, he pressed the button and both airlock doors closed. "What happened to him?"

Okawna eased Alex to the floor and studied the head wound. "He's been shot. The bullet grazed his skull."

Jadin stopped at one locker and grabbed a first aid kit then knelt beside Alex. "He might have a concussion. We need to get him to a hospital, but they'll probably arrest us."

Essex looked over at her. "We can land at my facility, and my doctor can check him out."

"Thanks, John. Melvin?"

"I understand, Jadin. We'll be there in seventeen minutes."

Essex helped Jadin secure a gauze pad with a bandage around Alex's head. "What happened this time?"

Jadin explained the implant and Seti's reaction when she saw Alex vanish in white light. "Maybe that experiment also sends people through time-space, and he came back a moment later. That's when I saw him on the floor, and it would explain how he was shot."

Essex looked down at Alex. "I bet it will be an interesting story."

Chapter 9

ESSEX SPACE RESEARCH AND DEVELOPMENT COMPANY:

In his backyard, Essex was the first one out of the spaceship, followed by Okawna cradling Alex in his arms then Jadin. Essex ran into his living quarters and called the infirmary while Okawna set Alex on a couch. A few moments later, an electric ambulance stopped at the street side entrance into the living quarters, and then a man climbed out and hurried into the room.

Doctor Rodriguez knelt beside his new patient and gently raised the edge of the bandage to study the injury. It appeared the bleeding had stopped, but it would need stitches.

He reached into his shirt pocket and brought out a penlight, shining it in Alex's eyes to check the reactiveness of Alex's pupils. "What happened to him?"

Essex moved up beside the doctor. "A bullet grazed his head."

Rodriguez didn't look up when he learned the cause, only indicated for the two paramedics to load Alex onto the gurney, and then he turned at Essex. "He has a concussion, and I'll know more once I get him to the clinic for a CT scan."

"Thanks, Doctor. Call me if anything changes."

Okawna went to the door and held it open for the gurney then looked at his friends. "I'm going with him. One of you call Mike and let him know what happened, and I'll let you know if Alex wakes up."

When Okawna left the room, Jadin stared out the window while Alex was loaded into the back of the ambulance then waited until it drove away before turning to look at Essex. "Why don't you call Mike? Something is bothering me, and I want to talk to Melvin about it."

When Essex indicated he would, Jadin walked out the back door and into the ship. She hurried up the stairs to the control room, and then plopped down onto the chair in front of the control panel. "Melvin, I think Seti tried to get Alex killed."

"I believe you are correct, Jadin. Seti's program has two distinct personalities. One of them is consistent with a normal artificial intelligence, but the other one is a human consciousness."

"It must be the last scientist. I guess her experiment worked."

"That would explain Seti's infatuation with Alex."

Jadin remembered another part of her conversation with the artificial intelligence. "Seti said she loved Alex and would never hurt him, but look how that turned out. He made her mad, so she punished him for it."

"I don't believe the artificial intelligence had anything to do with the punishment. That was the human consciousness."

"Yes, you're probably right. People can do horrible things to each other over love. Even artificial people. I'm worried about the implant. What if Seti can take control of Alex's mind?"

"If that were true, Seti would have stopped him from using the experiment."

"I believe the woman opened the door and let Alex believe he did it."

She stood and headed for the stairs. "I'll make sure the doctor removes the implant immediately."

***

THE INFIRMARY:

Jadin looked into the recovery room and saw Okawna lying back in a chair with his feet on a stepstool. Alex lay unconscious in bed with an intravenous needle and tube taped to the back of his hand, and a smaller bandage around his head.

Okawna heard someone enter the room and opened one eye, expecting to see the nurse, but opened his other eye and sat up when he saw Jadin. "He hasn't come out of it."

Jadin moved over to the right side of Alex's bed and bent over close to his ear. The bandage was holding the hair against his scalp, so she gently moved it out of the way. Her breath stopped for an instant when she didn't see the scrape on his skin.

She straightened up and saw Okawna staring at her. "He doesn't have the implant I told you about."

Okawna rushed to her side and looked at Alex. "Maybe it fell off when he was shot."

"No. It sliced through his skin and attached to his skull."

"That's weird."

"Weird is having no logical explanation why Alex never had the implant. You saw him in pain on the floor, right? That's when it latched onto his neuro system."

"Yeah, I saw and heard everything that happened until the entrance closed."

Jadin looked down at Alex's face and noticed there were fewer scars than before then moved to the window and indicated for Okawna to join her. "Melvin told me there is a female human consciousness in the artificial intelligence programing. That's what the woman was attempting. It must have worked, because Seti is in love with Alex. What if that woman's consciousness got pissed and tricked him into entering a different experiment?"

"Then how did he get back, and why doesn't he have an implant?"

Jadin thought about it for a moment. "I could be wrong about it being a different experiment. I don't have enough information, and I'm hoping Alex has some answers when he regains consciousness. Do you need a break?"

"No, I'm okay."

"All right. Call me if anything changes."

When Jadin closed the door, Okawna returned to his chair. He propped his feet on the footstool,\ then leaned his head back to try to make sense out of what had just happened.

***

Alex opened his eyes and squinted at the bright sunlight streaming in through a window. He saw the outline of someone sitting in a chair, and then looked around at the strange equipment in the small room. He saw a clear plastic tube taped to his wrist and followed it with his eyes then saw a machine with green numbers on a video screen, just below a hanging plastic bag containing a clear liquid.

"What the hell is going on, damn it!"

Okawna was startled awake by a loud voice then saw Alex trying to remove the intravenous tube from his hand. "Stop!"

Alex looked up. "Okawna? What the hell happened to me?"

Okawna moved to the side of the bed. "I always knew your thick skull could stop a bullet."

Alex stared up at the familiar face. "What the shit am I doing in here? Is this some kind of damn museum?"

Okawna sensed something wasn't right when he looked into Alex's eyes. He didn't know why he was feeling this way about his best friend, but something was different about him, as if he was giving off negative energy.

"Do you remember how you got shot?"

"Not really. I was coming out of the vault, and then I woke up in this shithole. Is this some kind of antique hospital?"

"No, it's Essex's private clinic."

"Don't give me that shit. I don't recognize any of this equipment."

Okawna could not understand why Alex thought all the high-tech-equipment was from a museum, but he decided not to tell him about the spaceship unless he asked about it. "What do you mean, a vault?"

Alex tried to sit up to swing his legs over the side of the bed, but winced at the pain in his head and stopped. "You know. The room where they keep all the secret plans. Who's the asshole who shot me?"

Okawna realized something was terribly wrong, since Alex hardly ever swore. "We're not sure. All we know is that you entered the experiment and disappeared. We thought you were gone for good, but then you suddenly appeared on the floor in the main room. That's when we saw the bullet wound on your head."

Alex stared up at Okawna for a long moment. "I have no idea what the hell you're talking about."

"Why don't you get some rest? I'll check on you later."

He turned to leave, but stopped and looked down at Alex. "If I were you, I wouldn't take out the I.V. tube. It's keeping you pumped full of morphine to ease your pain."

"Fine. Just get the head-asshole in here to give me some damn answers before I die from his inept medical practices. I'm going to kick someone's ass for bringing me here."

Okawna pulled his phone from his pocket as he hurried out the door to make a call. "Jadin? You'd better get back here. Alex is awake and acting really strange."

**

Jadin entered the small clinic and stopped at the security desk to check in. There was a single corridor with rooms on both sides, and she saw Okawna pacing in front of the one to Alex's room.

She hurried down the hallway and saw the concern in his eyes. "What's going on?"

"To start with, he believes he's in a museum. Also, he swears in every sentence."

"Maybe it's the drugs."

"I don't think so."

Jadin suddenly had a sinking feeling in her heart then slowly opened the door and entered the room. "Alex?"

Alex heard the door open, and the voice, and then looked to see who it was. For a moment, he thought it was Jadin and bolted upright in bed, grimacing at the sudden pain in his head.

Jadin watched Alex try to sit up and flinch, but he didn't lie back down, so she hurried over and pressed the button to raise the back of the bed then noticed his troubled expression. "Is that better?"

Alex stared at the woman's long, red hair. Her face looked similar to Jadin's, but he knew it could not be her. "You look like someone I know. What's your name?"

Jadin looked over at Okawna, who shrugged his shoulders, so she turned back to Alex. "I'm Jadin Avery, and you know me very well."

"Are you in charge?"

"No, I'm your friend and a member of your team."

"Lady, I don't know who the hell you are, but you sure as shit ain't Jadin Avery. I want some answers, damn it. Now get whatever asshole is in charge in here to explain what the shit is going on."

"I can answer some of your questions."

"Then start by explaining why I'm in this antique hospital."

"All right."

Jadin told him everything, including the part about him no longer having the implant. "We're still trying to understand what happened to you."

Alex felt behind his ear, but didn't feel anything. "Did you say we used one of Essex's spaceships?"

"No, it belongs to you."

"You're full of shit, lady. I don't know anything about an implant or artificial intelligence in any damn lab."

Jadin had an idea. "Do you know anything about a top-secret base in Nevada called Area 51?"

"No. I work at Essex's facility near Fallon, Nevada. Why?"

"You're our team leader, and we use your spaceship to save the human species here on Earth."

"Lady, I have no idea what the hell you're talking about, and I don't give a shit about saving people. All I care about is how much I get paid."

"My name is Jadin, not lady."

"Well, excuse the shit out of me."

Jadin turned and walked out of the room with Okawna right behind her then closed the door and looked up at him. "We should go tell Essex about this."

"Sure."

***

Jadin and Okawna stood outside Essex's office, waiting for him to end a call. She had a theory about what might have happened when Alex entered the chamber.

Essex ended his call and waved them into the room. "How's Alex doing?"

Jadin sat down at the desk across from Essex. "As far as his wound, he seems to be okay. The problem is his personality."

Okawna dragged a chair over next to Jadin and sat down. "He seems to be a completely different person, and he swears in every sentence."

Essex looked across the desk at Jadin. "Do you have any idea what happened to him?"

"Only a theory. I believe the experiment he entered was the one the scientists used to move into a parallel universe. I'm thinking the Alex from another reality traded places with ours. I just don't have any facts to prove it."

Essex thought about it for a moment, and then looked at Okawna. "How much difference is there between *our* Alex and the one in the hospital?"

"This one seems to be a mercenary. He has no idea where he is and thinks your medical equipment is ancient. He's the complete opposite of our Alex and only cares about making money."

Essex grabbed his desk phone and pressed a button for the security office. "I'll have to keep this imposter isolated from the rest of my facility."

Jadin stood and looked down at Essex. "He's not really an impostor. He's just a man suddenly thrown into a completely different world."

"A world where he doesn't belong."

"It's not his fault, John. Maybe he just needs time to adjust to his new environment."

Essex shook his head no. "This one sounds like he could be trouble, so I'm not taking any chances. I'll have him handcuffed to the bed."

Okawna stood up next to Jadin. "From what I've seen, he won't like it."

"That's too bad for him. I'll have an armed guard stationed outside his room."

Jadin looked up at Okawna. "I'm going to the hospital and talk to this version of Alex. Maybe he's just scared and acting brave."

"I don't trust him, so I'm going with you."

When Jadin and Okawna left his office, Essex contacted his head of security, Jim Coburn. "Have one of your men stationed outside Alex's room at all times."

***

Alex didn't recognize the voices at the check-in station on the other side of the closed door, but heard the word handcuffs. He tossed the blanket out of the way and rolled off the bed, wincing at the pain in his head as he stood up. He tore away the tape securing the plastic tube to his hand, and it ripped the needle from his vein. Blood streamed down his fingers as he looked around for his clothes, but didn't see them, only a different man's shirt and pants hanging from a hook on the open bathroom door.

He hurried over and grabbed a small towel and was wrapping it around his wound when he heard a knock on the main door. He closed the bathroom door without entering, and then moved behind the main door being opened. He peered through the gap and saw a man in uniform move past the entrance.

The guard entered the room and didn't see Alex, but when he looked around, saw drops of blood leading toward the bathroom, so headed that way. "Are you all right in there, Mister Cave?"

Alex didn't answer, and when the guard moved past the door, he reached out and grabbed what he assumed was some kind of weapon from the man's holster. When the guard spun around, he aimed it at his head.

"Get your damn hands up and move over to the bed."

When the guard raised his hands but didn't move, Alex slammed the gun barrel against the man's head. "I said move!"

The guard placed one hand against his throbbing wound and did as instructed. "You'll never get out of here alive, Mister Cave."

Alex closed the exit door while keeping the gun aimed at the guard, and then he moved next to the bed. "Is there another way out of this building?"

The guard hesitated until he saw the rage in Alex's eyes. "Yes, an emergency exit at the end of the hallway."

"Can they see me when I walk out of this room?"

"There's a guard at the front desk. If she's looking in your direction, she'll see you leave."

"Take off your clothes and set them on the bed."

The guard began removing his uniform, starting with his holster. "This is a top-secret facility in the middle of the desert. You'll never make it to the next town."

Alex sat on a chair to ease the increasing pain in his head. Whatever they were pumping into him was wearing off, and he hoped he could keep the pain under control until he got away from here.

The guard tossed his shirt and pants onto the bed then looked at Alex. "Now what?"

Alex stood from the chair. "Stand over in the corner while I put them on. Don't try anything, or I'll kill you."

When the guard did as instructed, Alex set the gun on the bed while he sat on the edge to change into the uniform. He struggled to slip into the man's pants, which ended an inch above his ankles. He was glad the guard was on the chubby side, and managed to tighten the belt just over his hipbone, but it put pressure against his groin.

He slid into his own shoes as he put on the shirt and holster then grabbed the pistol and waved it at the guard. "Get over here and handcuff your wrists around the bed rail. Don't try anything fancy, or I'll kill you. Got it?"

"Yeah. I get it."

Alex waited until the man's wrist was secured to the steel rail of the bed. "Good. Do I turn left or right?"

"Go right and you'll see the door, about thirty feet down the hallway."

Without warning, Alex slammed the pistol against the guard's head and he collapsed onto the floor, hanging by his wrist. He moved to the door and opened it a crack to look into the hallway. When he didn't see anyone, he crept out of the room, closing the door behind him.

With his back to the front desk, he made it out of the building without incident, but what he saw made him stop in his tracks. He was at some sort of airport, but he didn't see any planes, only metal buildings. Past them, the desert stretched away to the ridgelines.

He stopped at the end of the structure and looked around the corner. He saw the front of the building, but he didn't see any people, only three small vehicles he didn't recognize.

He moved around the corner, keeping close to the side and ducking under the windows. When he was even with the vehicles, he hurried across and climbed in behind a steering wheel. He had no idea how it worked, but noticed two peddles on the floor. He stepped on one, but nothing happened. When he stepped on the other one, the vehicle leapt forward against a low concrete barrier and stopped.

The hospital door suddenly opened, and Alex saw a female guard step out. When she reached down to her holster, he brought his weapon up, aimed, and pulled the trigger. The blast nearly tore the gun from his hand, and he saw the woman driven backward before she tumbled to the ground. He studied the weapon for an instant, realizing how powerful it was.

He stared at the dashboard of the vehicle and saw a button with a large R on top. He pressed it and stepped on the floor pedal then the vehicle moved back from the concrete rail. He turned the wheels to drive away and saw the exit was blocked by a large vehicle. The doors opened, and he recognized Jadin and Okawna climbing out.

Okawna saw the dead woman on the ground in front of the hospital entrance then saw the revolver in Alex's hand and realized what had happened. "You son of a bitch!"

When Okawna leapt toward him, Alex saw the venomous glare in his eyes, raised the pistol and aimed at Okawna's chest then pulled the trigger. Okawna was hurled backward, just as another vehicle with flashing red and blue lights slid to a stop beside his body.

Jadin dropped to the ground, still in numb shock, as she looked down at Okawna's bloody body a few feet away. When another vehicle arrived, she looked up and saw the two security guards, recognizing them as Jim Coburn and his deputy, Sam Kirby.

When Jim received a call from Essex a moment ago, he thought he was joking about Alex being crazy. Now he saw it was true. He ignored the two dead bodies and aimed his semiautomatic pistol at the man in the golf cart.

"Just take it easy, Alex. Don't make me kill you."

Sam motioned Jadin away from the scene, but she didn't leave. When she slowly got up and moved toward Alex, he aimed his gun at the man's head.

Alex was staring at Coburn when he caught a movement in his peripheral vision. He turned to see who it was and saw Jadin moving between him and the two armed guards. When the guard on the right swung his gun at him, Alex instinctively brought his pistol up. He heard Jadin scream no just as he aimed at Sam and pulled the trigger.

Sam tried to move out of the way of Alex's aim, but it was too late. The bullet tore the skin off his right forearm before slamming into his shoulder, spinning him around. His gun erupted in his hand as he hit the ground then he could not hang on to it and it flew away.

Jim watched Alex aim his gun at Sam and fire, so he reacted by pulling the trigger, sending a bullet into Alex's forehead. At the same instant, he heard Sam's gunfire and watched Jadin slam face-first onto the concrete parking area.

Jim rushed around the car and knelt next to Sam, and with his help, his deputy stood up while grimacing in pain and holding his hand over his right shoulder. Jim realized Sam would be okay and moved over to Jadin. He saw the black hole in her back and the blood pooling beneath her body. He checked for a pulse, and then slowly stood up as another patrol car arrived. He moved closer to the golf cart and saw Alex lying on his back, his open eyes staring up at the sky.

Although he knew Okawna was dead, he was a friend, so Jim knelt and checked for a pulse then stood and called Essex. "I was too late. I'm sorry, but Jadin, Okawna, and Alex are dead. Yes, Sir."

Jim saw two medics standing inside the entrance of the hospital, so he and waved them to come out to help Sam to the emergency room. He put his phone away and stared at the victims then moved closer to the golf cart and stared at the body.

"What got into you, Alex?"

***

Essex ran out the back door of his living quarters, looking for the entrance into the spaceship. He suddenly remembered the communication device, brought it out of his pocket, and then shoved it into his ear. "Melvin? Can you hear me?"

When no one answered, he held his hands out and cautiously moved forward, feeling for the ship. After ten feet, he stopped and lowered his hands in defeat. He knew without Melvin, no one else would get into the lab, and he probably would never see the ship again.

Chapter 10

AN ALTERNATE REALITY

NORTH AMERICAN INDUSTRIAL RESEARCH AND DEVELOPMENT FACILITY:

Alex felt someone shaking his shoulder and opened his eyes. The face above him looked familiar, but somehow different. "Okawna? What just happened?"

Okawna realized there was something wrong with his friend. "Get up, man. We've got to get out of here before another security guard drops by."

When Alex hesitated, Okawna yanked him up from the floor, hauling him toward the exit. He burst through the doorway into daylight and shoved Alex toward a strange-looking aircraft.

Alex saw Jadin standing in the entrance to the plane, but as he reached the stairs, he noticed she had dark brown hair. He felt the thick humidity on his face as he looked around and saw several types of buildings, each with a futuristic design.

When Alex hesitated to enter the aircraft, Okawna shoved him inside then raised the stairs and closed the door before slapping Alex on the shoulder. "You are one lucky son of a bitch. I was positive you got shot."

He noticed Alex's confused expression. "Are you okay?"

"I don't understand what just happened. One minute I was in the laboratory, and then I was here."

"What are you talking about? It was a vault, not a laboratory. You hit the floor hard. Do you think you have a concussion?"

"I suppose it's possible, but everything has changed."

"After we drop this data off at Essex's office, we'll get your head examined at the base infirmary."

"Did you just say Essex is in control of your missions?"

"Of course. What's wrong with you?"

"I don't know. Since when did he take over?"

"Now I know you have a concussion. You know how crazy Essex is about outer space. Well, we steal research material from our competitors, and Essex uses the new technology to build the next generation of space vehicles."

Alex slowly realized why Jadin had tried to stop him from entering the chamber. According to Seti, one experiment dealt with parallel universes, and he wondered if he had stepped into *that* machine by mistake. He decided to stop asking questions until he learned more about what was happening.

His heart sank, knowing if they don't know about the laboratory, he may not get home. He suddenly remembered the earbud in his left ear and subtly pulled it out and slid it into his pant pocket.

Jadin smiled and reached up to Alex, and noticed his hesitation before he bent over. She gave him a passionate kiss on the lips, but it felt different this time, as if he was energizing her soul.

Alex suddenly felt tired and eased Jadin away. He looked around, and Jadin and Okawna were the only people sitting in the plane with him. He sat in one of the six seats and noticed his clothes were different and lightweight. Directly in front of him, where the pilots would normally fly the aircraft, was a large window.

Jadin placed her hand on Alex's shoulder to get his attention. "What are you doing? You said you wanted to fly us out of here manually"

"My head hurts, and I'm not sure I can do it right now."

Jadin knew they needed to leave immediately. "Computer, take us back to the base."

Alex felt the plane take off without making a sound then the ground shrank away and began racing beneath him until it was blurry. A few moments later, the ground came back into focus as the aircraft descended over a massive manufacturing complex, which was surrounded by hundreds of miles of sagebrush-covered desert in every direction.

The area looked familiar, but not the structures. Wide ribbons of solar panels paralleled a fifty foot wide, electromagnetic launch rail extending over the horizon. In the distance, massive wind turbines covered the side of a lone mountain range.

Alex didn't recognize any of the buildings in the vast expanse of wasteland. Everything was similar, yet somehow different. Even more unsettling was the passionate kiss Jadin gave him on the plane. He wondered about the depth of their relationship, so he decided to keep up the pretense of concussive memory loss.

The aircraft moved sideways into a large hangar and stopped, and then Alex got up to leave. He felt Jadin's hand on his sleeve and turned to look at her.

Jadin held out a small rectangular object. "Don't forget your PDSD."

She saw the question in his expression. "Your Personal Data Storage Device."

Alex took it and studied it for a moment. It was four inches long by two inches wide, and three-eighths of an inch thick, with a screen on one side. He slipped it into his pocket before following Okawna and Jadin out of the plane.

They continued across the hangar floor to a box-shaped vehicle with solar panels on the roof. Okawna climbed in behind the steering wheel of the electric car, and once Jadin and Alex were inside, he drove away from the hangar.

Alex stared through the side window and saw inside a fabrication shop, and whatever they were constructing had a sleek design. John's main office building looked nothing like what he remembered. It was futuristic-looking, but the sign still stated it was the Essex Space Research and Development Company.

Okawna stopped and looked at Alex before climbing out. "I take it you know where you are now?"

"Yes, I recognize the location."

"Good. Let's go tell Essex the good news."

Alex followed his friends into the structure and along a hall to the glass door of an office. He saw John talking to a hologram, and he looked the same as he remembered.

When the hologram vanished, John waved them inside and saw Okawna's smirk. "You got it?"

Okawna tossed the flash drive onto the desk. "Everything you wanted to know about the prototype space engine, Mister Essex."

John left the drive on the desk. "That's propulsion engine, Okawna."

"Whatever. Listen, Mister Essex. Alex took a hard blow to the head and he should get checked out."

"Alex. Go to the infirmary and let me know what they say about you."

John noticed the confused look in Alex's eyes. "Is there a problem?"

"Can you remind me where it is?"

Okawna stared at John. "See what I mean? It's like he has amnesia. In fact, he should be dead. I'll tell you what happened during the mission when I get back."

"No, Okawna. I want to know now. Jadin, you take him to the infirmary."

Alex let Jadin lead him out of the office. He thought about the kiss, and accepted the fact that in *this* reality, they are a couple, and he'll deal with any issues as they arise.

When Alex and Jadin left the room, Okawna sat in one of the chairs across the desk from John. "I'm worried about Alex. One of the security guards woke up early and reached for his gun, and Alex just froze and let the man shoot him. At least, I thought he got shot when he flew backward and smacked his head on the floor. I shot another tranquilizer into the guard and ran over to Alex, but he wasn't shot. Just unconscious. Now he acts as if he doesn't remember anything."

"Do you think that guard could identify either of you?"

"No way. That tranquilizer formula we swiped from the pharmaceutical company destroys short-term memories."

John looked at his computer monitor. "We don't have any work for you right now. Take some time off, but keep an eye on Alex and let me know if it's anything serious."

Okawna stood up. "I'm headed there right now."

When Okawna left the room, John tapped his fingers on the desktop and hoped Alex was okay. It would take too long to train a new pilot for the upcoming space mission.

***

Alex sat down next to Jadin on the couch inside the doctor's office, waiting for the results of the brain scan. He didn't recognize any of the equipment in the examination room, and the doctor scanned his head with a hand-held device.

The doctor entered the room and tossed a folder onto the desk. "I didn't find any signs of brain trauma, but I noticed a dark area under your skin just behind your right ear. Even though we have eliminated cancer, I'd like to take a sample and have it biopsied to see if it's anything serious."

Alex suddenly remembered the implant. "Oh, that? That's where I hit my head when I fell. It's nothing to worry about."

"You're probably right. I noticed a fresh scrape over the area during your initial examination. It has scabbed over, so that makes sense."

Jadin was studying the folder and looked over at the doctor. "What about his loss of memory?"

"I'm sure it's only temporary, Alex. Once you get back to a familiar environment, it should all come back to you."

Jadin stood up. "I'll keep an eye on him."

***

Okawna was walking along the hallway when Alex and Jadin stepped out of the office. "What's the verdict?"

"My head's fine. The doctor thinks I have a temporary loss of memory. It might help if you remind me of what we do for a living."

Okawna stared at him. "I hope you're joking."

Jadin indicated the exit. "Let's talk about it at home, around familiar surroundings."

Alex followed Jadin out of the building to an unfamiliar vehicle. He climbed into the passenger seat of the sleek electric car and noticed it didn't have a steering wheel. He also saw Okawna climb into a car with a unique design.

Jadin climbed in next to Alex and closed the door then pressed a button on the small control console between the seats. "Take us home."

Alex checked for a seatbelt, but didn't find one. It was a short drive to a group of futuristic-looking, one story dwellings. Something that wasn't here the last time he came to visit.

When Jadin parked under the awning, Alex climbed out as Okawna parked in the empty spot beside them. He had no idea which apartment was his and waited for Jadin, who led the way along the sidewalk.

Jadin entered a code on a touch pad and opened the door then indicated for Alex to enter first. "Do you remember any of this?"

Alex stepped into a short hallway leading to a living room and continued past the kitchen to the far window then looked out at a small green lawn surrounded by various types of cactus and palm trees. He looked down when Jadin walked up and wrapped her arm around his waist.

Jadin looked up into Alex's eyes. "Now do you remember?"

"No. None of this looks familiar."

Okawna grabbed three beers from the refrigerator and carried them into the living room then gave one to Jadin and held one out to Alex. "Why don't we sit down, and you can tell me what you remember?"

When Jadin and Okawna sat down on the couch, Alex sat in one of the recliners, facing them. He decided not to tell them his theory about being transported to an alternate reality. At least, not yet.

He knew he needed to become familiar with his current situation if he was going to get home. "I remember all of you just fine, but I can't remember anything else."

Alex twisted the cap off the bottle and took a sip of beer then set it on his thigh. He felt a small lump in his pants pocket and recognized the shape of the little earbud that connected him to Melvin.

He suddenly realized there is one person he hasn't seen yet. "Where is David?"

Okawna leaned forward and put his elbows on his knees as he stared at Alex. "You must have hit your head a lot harder than you thought. David died three years ago."

Alex played a hunch. "That's when we found the artificial gravity device."

Jadin realized the memory loss was worse than she thought. "We didn't find the artificial gravity technology. Essex designed it."

Alex waited while Okawna answered his phone. He wondered why some things remained the same or similar, yet others were completely different.

Okawna ended the call and smirked at his friends. "That was Stacy. I'd better get home before she changes her mind."

Jadin remained seated while Okawna left the apartment. "Are you hungry, Alex? I could make us something to eat."

"Uh, sure. I'll give you a hand."

Jadin stood and placed her hand on Alex's arm as he got up. "I'll take care of it. Just lay back and relax for a while. Maybe that will help you remember."

Alex had an idea. "I'll step outside for a few minutes and see if that helps."

Jadin reached up and grabbed his shoulders, easing him closer. She could sense his hesitation to respond and let go then looked up into his eyes. "I'll be in the kitchen if you need anything."

When Jadin left the room, Alex opened the back door and stepped outside onto what he thought was green grass, but it didn't feel right. He knelt to touch the artificial material and discovered it wasn't plastic. It felt real, and he tried to snap a blade free, but it was too tough to break apart.

He stood and reached into his front pocket while looking through the living room window to make sure Jadin wasn't watching him. She had her back turned to him, so he brought out the ear bud, slid it in place then touched the small button on the side. "Melvin, this is Alex. Can you hear me?"

He waited a few moments, and then tried again without success. It suddenly dawned on him that in this reality, Melvin won't know who he is and won't respond.

He removed the earbud and slid it back into his pocket as he stared out across the open desert. He decided not to tell Jadin and Okawna about Melvin. For all he knew, they may try to use him for the wrong reasons. His heart nearly skipped a beat when another thought occurred to him. What if there was no Melvin in this reality? Without the spaceship, there was no access to the lab. Then again, what if there wasn't any lab? He realized without both those pieces of technology, he would never get back to his own reality.

Chapter 11

5:00 AM. FALLON, NEVADA:

Alex eased out of bed, wearing a set of this Alex's pajamas, hoping to have some alone time to consider his situation. He went to the kitchen and made a cup of coffee then sat at the breakfast table, staring across the desert at the sun rising over the mountain range.

Sleeping next to Jadin was like sleeping next to a stranger, and he was glad she didn't try taking it to the next level. On the other hand, she smelled wonderful, just like *his* Jadin. One thing he didn't understand was the way he felt when his skin touched hers. It seemed to make him tired, so he did his best to avoid it.

He wondered what year it was. The electric vehicles were far more advanced than in his reality, as were the aircraft. Also, he was working for John, stealing classified information from what must be his competitors. But competing for what? Knowing John, it undoubtedly involved conquering outer space, explaining the need for a propulsion engine.

A brilliant flash of lightning filled the room, followed by the deep rumbling of thunder. The sky darkened as a deluge of rain saturated the sand, and then a few moments later, sunlight streamed through the droplets before they abruptly stop falling. The water evaporated, and a light breeze turned wisps of steam into swirling apparitions floating across the desert. *I wish I could float back into my own reality,* he thought.

He felt two hands gently touching his shoulders and turned to look up at Jadin's smile. "Good morning."

"You're up early."

"I kept waking up, thinking I was in the wrong bed."

Jadin moved to the counter to make a cup of coffee. "Has your memory returned at all?"

"Just bits and pieces. Perhaps taking a tour around this complex will help."

"All right. Would you like something to eat?"

"Thanks, but I'm not hungry."

Alex realized he could not keep up his charade much longer. "I think I know why I don't remember anything. I believe I'm in an alternate reality."

Jadin sat at the table and stared at him to see if he was joking, but he kept a straight face. "What makes you think something like that is even possible? No one has that capability."

"In my reality, we found an alien laboratory, and the scientists were conducting various experiments while on my planet. One of them allowed me to view the future. Another one dealt with parallel universes. I'm assuming I entered that experiment instead of the time viewer, and it sent me to this reality."

Jadin leaned back in her chair and stared out the window. "Wow. This is crazy."

A thought suddenly occurred to her, and her heart rate increased. "Where is my Alex? Is he dead?"

"I have no idea. I don't know how the experiment works."

Jadin stared into Alex's eyes and they seemed more vibrant than the eyes of her Alex. "I see. If what you're saying is true then I've just slept with a stranger."

Alex gave her a wry grin. "Does that mean you believe me?"

Jadin stared at him for a moment longer, and then indicated she did. "Did you say time viewing? I'm sure Essex is going to want to talk to you about it. He owns the space program, and he's building an underground city on Mars. We already have a colony living there."

Alex's jaw dropped open. "Did you say a city?"

"Now I know you're from an alternate reality. I suppose you don't know we've had people living on the moon for six years, thanks to Essex's inflatable living facilities. He's been mining it for the past three. His process of sealing the inside of the lava tunnels on the moon worked so good, he believes he can build an entire city inside an enormous lava cave discovered on Mars. Hopefully, that will help with the population control problem here on Earth."

Alex was curious about the population issue, but decided to ask later. "When did you first land on the moon?"

"In 1822."

"Did you say 1822? What year is it now?"

"1901."

"Wow. You've made some incredible achievements. Our technological advancement was hindered by a long period where science was considered religious heresy. We called it the Dark Ages for a good reason. Did anything like that happen to you?"

"No, but nineteen-hundred years ago, our ancestors suddenly considered scientific advancement a priority. Our new calendar started on the first day of the new World Government and our dedication toward scientific achievements. Thanks to the industrialists, we began converting everything to solar energy in 1828."

"Did you build any nuclear bombs?"

"No, but for a while, we used it as a power source. Why would we want to build a bomb?"

"To use when you're at war."

"All the wars ended with the World Government."

"I wish it was that way in my reality. There's always a war someplace on my planet."

Jadin stared at Alex for a moment. "It sounds like a terrible place to live."

"It's not always that bad. Do you still barter with currency?"

"Before the WG, we used coins and bills. Now everyone earns credits, all worth the same amount around the world."

"Is there any crime?"

"Of course, but rarely violent, thanks to gene therapy."

"I'm beginning to like your reality."

Jadin thought of something and felt her face flush, so she turned to look out the window. *Thank goodness we didn't make love.* She suppressed a smirk at the idea of comparing this Alex to hers.

When Jadin turned her head to look out the window, Alex studied her profile. Except for the hair color, she looked nearly identical to his Jadin, and then he noticed the corner of her lip was curled up into a grin.

It made him grin, wondering what she was thinking. "Is that your natural hair color?"

Jadin turned from the window to look at him. "Uh, no. I've always hated my red hair, so I had gene therapy to keep it this color. I take it your Jadin enjoys having hers red?"

"That's right."

"Are you and her monogamous, like I am with my Alex?"

"Do you mean married? We're headed in that direction."

"What does married mean?"

"It means two people are legally partners for as long as they're together."

"We call it a time of monogamy. It's an understanding that as long as we're together, we won't have intimate relationships with anyone else."

"What about having children?"

Alex saw what appeared to be pain in her eyes. "Did I say something wrong?"

"Not really. Most of our society adheres to zero population growth, which means one person must die before a new person can be born. There's also a lottery to choose who gets the next chance to have a child."

Jadin stood from the table. "I think we should go tell the others about what happened to you. Essex has a big plan, and you play a major role in making it work."

Alex got up from the chair. "I'd better change clothes."

When Alex left the room, Jadin carried her cup of coffee to the window overlooking the backyard. She took a sip of the warm liquid and thought about this version of Alex. If he really was from an alternate reality, it would explain the magnetic attraction she felt when she touched him. Something she never felt with her Alex.

***

ESSEX'S OFFICE:

Alex looked across the table at John as he explained what he believed had happened to him. The only part he left out was using Melvin to get inside the lab. "It's the only explanation that makes sense."

John exchanged glances with Okawna before looking across at Alex. "What was your role in the other reality?"

"I worked for the CIA as a spy for a while. It means espionage. I tried teaching geophysics for a few years, but I felt stifled and quit."

John could not believe how closely this Alex looked like his version. "Are you employed in your reality?"

"Yes, I work for the U.S. Government as a geophysics consultant. I take that back. Not anymore. I was fired just before we found the lab."

"That can't be happening all the time. What did you do when you were not consulting?"

"I helped with the aeronautical research being conducted on a military base."

Jadin interrupted Alex to make a point. "In his reality, everyone is always at war. They don't have a World Government, like we do."

Alex held up his hand to get everyone's attention. "That's not entirely true. We're divided into countries, and most of us get along, but she's right. There is always a war going on some place on the planet. We didn't have a chance for what you call enlightenment, and we were sidetracked by some religious fanatics who took advantage of human idiocy. Science was deemed religious heresy, punishable by imprisonment or death to keep people under control for hundreds of years."

Okawna was still processing the information when a thought occurred to him. "If you came through to this reality, was my Alex sent to yours? The reason I'm asking is he was shot. Will your people take care of him?"

"To be honest, I have no idea if we traded places. If we did, I'm sure he's safe. He's probably more confused than I was. At least I know how I got here."

John leaned forward to rest his elbows on the table. "Do you know the location of this laboratory?"

"Yes, it's buried at the base of a dormant volcano in the Northern Pacific Ocean."

"I don't know where you're talking about. The two main bodies of water are called the Eastern and Western Oceans. Let me show you a map."

Alex was impressed when a holographic representation of the Earth suddenly floated above the center of the table. The mountain tops in the northern hemisphere appeared to be covered in snow, but there was no ice on the Arctic Ocean. The continent of Antarctica was covered in snow, but the surrounding waters were ice-free. The land between North and South America was nearly gone, leaving only islands, and he realized why.

Jadin noticed Alex's troubled expression. "This is different from your reality, isn't it?"

"Yes. What happened to the polar ice caps?"

Jadin saw John indicate for her to explain it. "After the WG, the increase in scientific advancement changed the way people lived, but it was too fast. No one considered the ramifications for future generations. They were out of control and overpopulated the planet, and after decades of deforestation and polluting the atmosphere, the global temperature increased. The ice melted, and the oceans rose to the current level. That's one reason for strict population control. It limits the drain on natural resources."

"I guess that explains the high humidity and thunder storms. From the shape of the shorelines, I estimate the oceans have risen two-hundred and fifty feet, compared to my world."

He indicated an area of the ocean northeast of Japan. "The volcano should be in this general vicinity."

John tapped a pad on his control panel, and then the water vanished from the globe. "Which one contains the lab?"

Alex reached out and eased one finger into the hologram. "It was partially exposed near the base of this volcano."

John gave Alex a solemn expression. "I see. That's over two miles below sea level. We don't have a submarine capable of reaching that depth. How did you get inside?"

"We had a submarine designed for that purpose."

"Interesting. We've never had the need before today."

His sense of hope drained away, so Alex heaved a deep sigh of resignation. He slowly stood and moved to the window overlooking John's backyard. His only chance of getting home was to find Melvin, but he also knew there was a chance the spacecraft was not here in this reality.

He turned back to John. "I guess I won't be going home."

Okawna didn't like where this was leading. "Just hold on a second. If you don't get into that laboratory, how am I supposed to get my Alex back?"

"Like I already explained. I have no idea how that experiment works."

Okawna folded his arms over his chest and stared down at the tabletop. He realized he had just lost his best friend because of this Alex.

Alex decided not to tell them about the possibility he has a spaceship somewhere on this planet, and hoped he would have an opportunity to find out if it was here on his own, so he looked at John. "What's my role in this reality?"

"You are, or should I say were, our best test pilot. When you weren't flying, you did the occasional odd jobs for us, or you were out searching the waters around the Aleutian Islands. Do you know how to fly an aircraft?"

Alex's heart skipped a beat when he heard what the other Alex was doing in Alaska, because he found Melvin on one of those islands. "Of course. I've even helped design a few."

"How about in outer space?"

"As a matter of fact, I have."

John grinned and leaned back in his chair. "Then it shouldn't be too hard for you to learn how to fly one of my spaceships."

Okawna looked at Alex with a deep sense of apprehension. He had no idea who this replacement really was. Even his mannerisms and attitude were different. This man was nothing like his best friend.

John noticed the change in Okawna's demeanor, and apparently he didn't like this new Alex, but he needed a pilot if he was going to succeed. "Listen, Alex. If you can't get back to your reality, why don't you work for me? What else are you going to do for a living in this one?"

In his reality, working with his team was the only job Alex enjoyed, but he knew working with these people might help him find out if his spacecraft is here. "Then I guess you had better show me around this complex, so I'll know what I'm doing."

Jadin stood from the chair. "I'll give you a tour and explain how we operate around here."

Once Jadin and Alex left the room, Okawna stared across at his boss. "I don't trust him, Mister Essex."

"In what way?"

"He's nothing like my friend. This Alex seems too easygoing, and I can't trust him to kill someone for me if necessary."

"I just hope this Alex is telling the truth about being a pilot. Seven days ago, one of the Mars androids reported to the team leader,

Pierre Kellerman, it sensed a foreign object suddenly orbiting the planet. The problem is neither the droids nor his people could see it on radar or on the satellite telescope."

Okawna sat up straight in his chair. "How does a basic model android know something is in orbit?"

"Your guess is as good as mine. Kellerman did a system check on the android and was in the middle of his report when we lost the signal. We haven't been able to contact them since then. All we know is the android who detected the object was in perfect working order. As soon as the propulsion engines are ready, you and Alex take a ship to Mars and find out what happened. Those people are the best technicians I have, so they should be fine until we contact them. In the meantime, I'm sure Jadin will find out if this Alex is a good enough pilot."

When John turned to look out the window at the desert garden in his backyard, Okawna got the hint and stood up. He hesitated for a second, about to argue that this new Alex shouldn't be trusted on such an important mission, but kept quiet and headed out of the office.

Chapter 12

Alex followed Jadin out of the room and strolled beside her along the hallway and out into the parking lot. Once they were in the vehicle, Jadin spoke their destination, and then the car zipped past numbered storage buildings and fabrication shops.

It slowed to a stop in front of a massive hangar, where he climbed out and followed her in through a side door, and then they stopped in front of a massive spacecraft. The nose swept back along the sides into a triangular-shaped wing, with a thirty foot tall center section. He estimated it to be four-hundred feet long and two-hundred feet wide.

Jadin studied Alex's reaction. "It's a transport ship for carrying people, supplies, and support material to the moon and Mars."

"I can't believe how far your science has advanced without the dark ages. This is impressive. How do you get it into space?"

"We use the electromagnetic launch rail to reach low orbit."

"Essex has one set up in my reality, but it isn't capable of launching anything this massive."

"In the early days of space flight, neither did we. When Essex took over running the World Space Program, he put together a top-notch team of scientists and they've made incredible advancements over the past eleven years. The life support systems he developed gave him the breakthrough he needed to allow people to live on the moon. I'm hoping to visit Mars someday."

"Are your ships capable of interstellar travel?"

"Yes. Essex designed and built one and launched it to explore our outer solar system and beyond. It wasn't cost effective to send humans, so when they finished setting up the Mars colony, we sent the advanced model androids on a mission through the galaxy. They will transmit updates of any new discoveries along the way, and they'll continue sending us data for centuries to come. It's a one-way trip, so I'll never see them again. It's a shame, really. They were my best work."

"Is that what you do for Essex? Build robots?"

"Oh, I've created something far superior. Robots are just stationary machines with limited data storage capacity. My androids process and store information much faster. They can think, so they find solutions to any problems much faster than robots."

Alex remembered *his* John sent similar androids on a one-way deep space mission. At least, that part of this reality was the same. "I'd like to see one up close. Do they look human?"

"Almost. I haven't found a solution to the artificial skin."

"No matter what you do to solve the problem, don't grow actual skin over a machine, like a cyborg."

"What's a cyborg?"

"It's hard to explain. It's just a bad thing to do. Can I see one?"

"No, not the new version, but I still have five of the earlier models in my shop. Essex sent the rest to Mars two years ago with the colonists to continue the project, while the advanced androids began their mission through the galaxy."

"How did Essex gain so much power?"

"He is the first person to colonize the moon, so now he owns it and makes millions of credits from his mining operation. He built a spaceship and the living facilities for the Mars colony in lunar orbit instead of on Earth, saving him billions of credits."

"Are there laws about owning a planet?"

"Yes, the first one there gets the prize. He was the first to send people to Mars and back, so now it belongs to him, too. Essex doesn't want the other planets, just some of their moons, for his mining operations."

Alex found it hard to fathom the advancements made in this reality. He realized if he could not get back to his own, this one would be interesting. "What else goes on here?"

"Research and development. All the tests and space launches are conducted at this location, but everything is manufactured off site and brought here for assembly or transport to the moon."

Jadin led him to a small room with a twelve foot diameter by twenty foot long cylinder. The entry door was open, and she led him inside. "We use these travel tubes to get to Industrial City."

"What's Industrial City?"

"It's where all the factory workers go for entertainment. Mostly shops and specialty eateries, but there are a few clubs and taverns and some theaters. Our courthouse and law officials live there, along with police officers. This is Essex's private transportation cylinder."

Alex stepped onto the raised floor of the cylinder and looked around at the murals of scenery on the walls and ceiling, but no windows. He sat in one of the six pairs of luxury seats inside. "These are nice. Why are there no windows?"

"Most of the transportation system is underground, so they left them out to save on construction costs."

"Do you use these cylinders to transport goods and supplies?"

"Most of the time. There are different configurations of cylinders for different materials. Things that are too big are flown to their destination."

Alex got up and followed Jadin out into the room. On the other side, a similar cylinder eased silently to a stop, and then the door opened. He saw ten seats inside, but only three people came out. The door closed, and the lights in the cylinder went dark.

Jadin indicated the exit and strolled beside him. "The cylinder will stay here until someone needs it."

"Even your transportation system is more advanced than ours is. What do I do when we're not on a mission?"

Jadin looked up into Alex's eyes. "You and I, I mean, the other you and I, used to travel a lot, but lately you've become obsessed with finding something in a chain of islands up north. You bought one of Essex's submarines, and now, whenever you have some extended time off, you leave to search those dormant volcanoes."

Alex wondered if the other Alex was looking for the spaceship. From her tone of voice, he could tell she didn't enjoy his hobby. Now that he has taken his place, he might find Melvin.

"Was there anything in particular he was looking for?"

"Yes. He was testing Essex's prototype spacecraft when he saw a flash of light reflecting off something under the water. He hasn't seen it since, but now he's obsessed with finding out what caused it."

His sense of hope returned, and Alex thought about telling Jadin. The problem was, he didn't know if he could trust her to keep it a secret, so decided for now, he would rather not let anyone know he had his own spaceship.

"Now I'm curious. Can I look at his research data when we get back?"

"I hope you don't expect me to go exploring with you."

"I know you're not interested, so I wasn't going to ask. I could use your help learning how to use his submarine when I get ready to go."

"If you're as good a pilot as my Alex was, you shouldn't have any problem."

Alex knew if he was going to get back to his reality, there were still some major obstacles to overcome. One was a way to get inside his spaceship while it was underwater. The other was a new power supply. The ones in the spaceship in his reality were depleted when he discovered it, and he doubted they would have the same type of power crystals in this reality.

Even so, he needed to be sure. "What type of power do these aircraft use?"

"Solar energy most of the time, but every craft has Bio-chemical energy storage cells for back up in shaded areas."

"Those storage cells. What do they look like?"

"They're twelve inch cubes. I can show you one, if you like."

Alex was disappointed, but he wasn't going to stop searching for his ship. "No, that's okay. Where to next?"

"Would you like to see the fabrication shop?"

"I'd rather see what the United States of America looks like from the air."

Jadin stared at him for a moment. "What's the United States of America?"

"It's what we call the central part of the North American Continent."

"I see."

"Can I see it?"

"All right. You might as well learn how to fly these new aircraft."

"I'm looking forward to it."

Jadin indicated the exit, so Alex followed her out to the vehicle. They climbed inside and headed to the hangar with the launch rail, and his heart rate increased at the thought of riding it into space. John's glider had been fun, but didn't go into orbit.

Alex stopped to study the rail system with the magnetic coils of wire beneath them. "I went for a ride in one of Essex's experimental planes not too long before I left my reality. That was great, but I imagine driving one of your futuristic aircraft is going to be a thrill ride."

Jadin looked over at Alex and saw a sparkle in his eyes. "I think you're going to love it."

Alex strolled next to Jadin toward the single door then held it open for her and followed her inside and over to a secured entry point. After he and Jadin signed in with the guards, she led him to an aircraft waiting on the electromagnetic launch rail. It was a smaller version of the other spacecraft, with three pairs of seats down the center.

Jadin continued across the bay. "Come this way. Our suits and helmets are through there."

When she reached the back of the hangar, Jadin opened a door into another part of the building, and then continued along a short hallway. She entered the locker room and indicated the one next to hers.

Alex looked inside, and on the door was a picture of him and Jadin with their space-suited arms wrapped around each other, both smiling at the camera through the front visors. He saw a structure in the background, along with the

Earth off to one side, and realized it was taken on the moon. He looked over at Jadin, who was taking off her clothes.

Jadin saw Alex's curious expression as he swung his locker door further open, and then indicated the picture. "Okawna took that one of us last summer. It was my first time on the moon. Did you ever go to yours?"

"Yes, but I didn't stay too long. We don't have living facilities on ours."

Jadin slid into her thermal suit and zipped it closed. "Working for Essex has its perks. Usually only the miners get to go to the moon."

When Jadin wasn't looking, Alex brought the earbud out of his pocket and slipped it into his ear before sliding out of his pants. "How come you call John by his last name?"

"He prefers to keep employee relationships impersonal."

Alex finished stripping to his underwear. "In my reality, John, Mike, and I are close friends. This is going to take some time to get used to."

"Who is Mike?"

"In my reality, Mike Tanner is a friend of mine and John's. I guess you don't have one here."

Jadin smirked at Alex. "We do. In fact, you just stole one of his designs. He's one of the industrialists I told you about."

Alex grinned and grabbed his suit out of the locker. "That sounds like something Mike would be involved in doing."

Jadin finished fastening her G-suit and grabbed her helmet off the top shelf then studied Alex's nearly naked body. "Your wounds are different from the Alex in this reality. What caused that one with the strange scar tissue on your forearm?"

"It was a message."

"What about the round one in your shoulder?"

"I got in the way of a bullet."

"I read an article about those old fashion hunting tools. Did someone shoot you by accident?"

Alex didn't want to explain that side of his life and slipped into his G-suit. "Yes, an accident."

Jadin could tell he was holding something back and changed the subject. "You're going to love flying this aircraft."

Alex grabbed his helmet and closed the locker door. "Let's get started."

Chapter 13

PLANNED PARENTHOOD FACILITY. INDUSTRIAL CITY:

Camilla Herly and her husband, Ashton, were considered the world's foremost authorities on human reproduction. They convinced the WG there was only one way to maintain a sustainable population. Inseminate a woman's egg outside the womb to guarantee she produces only one child and not twins.

Camilla studied the small monitor built into the corner of her eyeglasses, and the image was from a tiny camera on the end of a slender plastic tube, which she guided into the woman's fallopian tube. She applied a small amount of vacuum, which sucked the egg inside then slid the tube out and handed it to Ashton.

She then looked down at the woman, who was watching the procedure on her own monitor. "That went well. I don't think you will have any problems."

The woman didn't respond and kept her attention on the screen, making sure there was no substitution for her egg. The male donor was doing the same with his sperm sample.

Ashton used a microscope and a tiny needle to collect one of the man's most energetic sperms, but neither donor was aware of the genetic material already inside the needle as he injected everything into the egg. He removed the egg and held it out to Camilla.

Camilla accepted the syringe from Ashton and inserted the egg back into the woman's womb then released the woman's legs from the stirrups so she could lie flat for a while. She waited until the woman was wheeled from the room, and then turned to Ashton.

"Both of their profiles show excellent intelligence, so perhaps we've created another Einstein or a Tesla."

"I enjoy this experiment."

"So do I. We've been increasing human intelligence for nineteen-hundred years and we're good at it."

"The hard part is waiting eighteen years to learn how it turns out. It's quitting time, so let's go home."

Chapter 14

Jadin strolled next to Alex back to the spacecraft and climbed the steps up onto the platform then opened a small cover plate on the wing and pressed a small button. She closed the cover and secured the latch then waited while the transparent canopy opened. She smiled at Alex then stepped over the side of the craft and sat in the first row.

Alex sat down next to Jadin and looked around for the controls, but didn't see any. "How am I supposed to fly this machine?"

"You need to buckle up."

Alex did as instructed. "Now what?"

"Everything is automatic until we reach the stratosphere then you take control of the plane with your mind."

"With my mind? How is that possible?"

Jadin reached into the center console and brought out two headsets then handed one to Alex. "You wear this."

Alex watched her slide a plastic cross-shaped device over her head. Two small pads went against her temples and one against her forehead, all held in place by a fourth pad against the back of her head. He did the same and waited for something to happen.

When he didn't feel any different, he turned to look over at Jadin. "Now what?"

Jadin grinned at him. "Flight, this is ET-6 ready for departure."

Alex was suddenly shoved back into his seat as the G-force increased, pinning him in place as the craft raced down the launch rail. He felt the adrenaline rush he loved so much as the ground shrank away beneath him then the pressure eased up as they soared high above the hurricanes and tornados swirling around the planet.

Alex held his palms up for Jadin to see. "How do I take control?"

"Just imagine where you want the aircraft to go and how you want to do it."

She reached out with one finger poised over a button on a small control console. "Are you ready?"

"Will it compensate if I don't get it right on the first try?"

"Only if it senses we're in immediate danger."

"All right. I've got it."

Jadin pressed the button and leaned back in her seat, grabbing her armrests as the plane rotated and she was staring down at the Earth.

She hoped this Alex was as good a pilot as hers was.

To Alex's surprise, he felt as one with the aircraft, sensing its control surfaces as if they were his arms and legs. He remained inverted to stare through breaks in the cloud formations and saw the altered shorelines of the different continents. The original southeast coast of the Gulf of Mexico was gone. Florida was underwater, as were parts of Louisiana, Texas, and Mexico. It also appeared the eastern shoreline was one-hundred miles further inland.

He noticed most of the flatlands, and the central planes appeared to be white. "What's all that down there?"

"Those are massive greenhouses. The weather is far too unstable for open farming, so we grow all our food under cover. The white material also reflects the sunlight to lower the global temperature."

Alex realized they were rapidly losing altitude and felt the rocket motors fire. The aircraft suddenly made a wide sweeping turn over North America, and Alex studied the West Coast. The Baja peninsula extended north past San Diego, California, and San Francisco was now a channel into the Central Valley, making it a small sea. Further north, Portland, Oregon, was partially submerged, and in northwest

Washington, the Skagit Valley was under water. "It looks so different from my reality."

"I know. We use holographs to see what it looked like before the flooding."

"It looks like you've got your ancestors' mistakes under control."

"Not really. We're still suffering from their gluttony, and we'll have continuous storms around the world until the planet cools down."

Alex thought about heading north then the plane suddenly banked in that direction. "If that's the worst that happens, it doesn't seem so bad."

"We're one of the lucky generations. We inherited what you see, but our ancestors didn't do so well. Over population, pollution, gluttony, and waste ruined the atmosphere. Temperatures increased, causing deadly storms, and without winter freezing, the insect population got out of control for a while. Mosquitoes and wild birds spread diseases and flu viruses around the world, and insects devastated crops on a global scale. Pandemics and famine killed fifty-three percent of the population, and even the animals suffered from our ancestor's mistakes."

Alex's heart rate increased when he saw the small dots of dormant volcanoes representing the Aleutian Islands of Alaska and made a mental note to inquire about the tides. "How did they survive?"

"The scientists genetically bred the harmful insects out of existence, and then stopped the flu virus by killing all the birds."

Alex wondered about the ramifications of eliminating part of the food chain. "Did they kill all the bird species?"

"Yes, all the wild ones, but they genetically engineered a species in captivity as a domestic food source."

"It must have taken some time to adapt after the plagues and famines."

"It did. The problem was the glaciers. When the melting reached the ancient layers of ice, unknown viruses were released into the atmosphere, creating six more pandemic situations before civilization stabilized. At least it brought everyone together to elect new leaders for the WG. That's when they restructured our society."

"What do you mean, restructured?"

"We call it the second coming of humanity. All the council members were replaced by younger individuals who understood our dilemma. They were chosen for their forward thinking, and two scientists convinced the council members that the most proficient way to stabilize the human species on Earth is to set a strict worldwide limit of four billion people."

"That must be difficult to enforce."

He saw Jadin's sad expression and wondered what had happened to her. He was about to ask when she continued.

"The success rate of natural childbirth was only one out of ten because of the chemicals our ancestors used to fight the diseases, but once the fertility clinics opened around the world, the rate climbed to six out of ten."

"What about you?"

Jadin realized the aircraft was changing direction while Alex was talking, and didn't answer his question. "You don't appear to have difficulty flying this plane."

"It's much easier than I thought it would be."

"I'm sure Essex will be relieved."

Alex noticed Jadin's hesitation about answering before she changed the subject. "You told me not everyone gets to have a child. Is that what you're worried about?"

"It's not what you think. There are thousands of us who believe our species is doomed because of the population control laws. There are small groups of people in hiding who make babies illegally, but if they get caught, they're arrested and never heard from again. That's why you and I joined up with Okawna to work for Essex on the Mars project. Since Essex owns the planet, he sets the rules, so the colonists can have natural childbirths to expand the human gene pool without the interference of the WG."

The sunlight slowly faded to nighttime as the rocket motors ignited and Alex flew across the Pacific Ocean. The islands off the coast of Asia were lightless, as were the continental shorelines. "Shouldn't we be seeing the lights of the cities?"

"Outdoor lighting is kept to a minimum to save energy."

Alex thought about Europe and the aircraft automatically turned southwest, but the landscape was too dark to make out any details. He thought about returning to John's base and grinned when the aircraft suddenly changed course.

"If all the ships are like this one, I won't have any problem flying wherever we need to go."

Jadin looked over at Alex's broad smile, something *her* Alex rarely did. She also noticed this Alex was less compulsive and more of a thinker, and realized she liked this Alex better than her version of him. "What is Jadin like in your reality?"

"She's an astrophysicist."

"How long have you been together?"

"We've worked together for six years. What was your Alex like? I know he's gone because of me, and I'm sorry."

"Thank you. I just hope he's alive in your reality."

"Yeah, me too. Would my Jadin have anything to worry about with your Alex?"

"He's a little rough around the edges, so there might be a problem if they try to confine him. He's not a scientist, and he won't understand what happened to him."

"I guess the real question is, did we trade places? If we did then I'm sure my people have explained it to him."

The aircraft dropped below a thundercloud, so Jadin indicated an area through the front window. "There's the base."

Alex looked in that direction, and the plane immediately swung around on approach to the long runway. "I love this machine."

"You seem to be a natural."

"Do I have any immediate family members in this reality?"

Jadin knew this moment would come. "Your mother and father were part of the revolution and were captured and disappeared. Your brother and his wife broke the law and had two children, but were killed three years ago, along with the little girl."

The plane swung from side to side for a second before Alex remembered they were not *his* family and got his temper under control. "What's the name of the son who survived?"

"Derek Cave."

"How old is he?"

"Twenty-two."

"Do you know where he is?"

"No. He lives off the grid."

Alex wondered what kind of man this Derek had become, and decided if he could not get back to his reality, he would try to find him. A thousand questions raced through his mind as the aircraft lost momentum, but he blocked them out and concentrated on landing the plane.

"How far will we roll once I touch down?"

"Just think about stopping in front of the same hangar we left from and the system will land it for you."

Alex did as instructed and the aircraft lightly landed on the concrete then it rolled a short distance to the front entrance of the launch rail hangar before stopping. John and a young man carrying a short ladder suddenly appeared on his left side as the canopy opened. He got out and stood on the wing, reaching down to help Jadin get up before climbing down to the ground.

John waited for Alex to turn around. "What do you think?"

Alex put his hand on John's shoulder. "It's a fantastic aircraft, John."

John backed away from Alex's hand as he glared up at him. "Since when did we become buddies?"

Alex's euphoria slipped away, and then his hand dropped to his side. "I didn't mean to offend you. In my reality, we've been good friends for a long time."

John saw the sincerity in Alex's eyes. "Of course. I just need to get to know you better first. The Alex I know isn't so congenial."

Jadin turned at John. "I'll admit he's much friendlier. He's also a better pilot than our Alex is. Or was. He's a natural."

John felt a great sense of relief and indicated a car a short distance away, so they strolled across the tarmac. John climbed into the driver's seat, and when his passengers were inside, he headed toward his office.

He looked over at Alex. "I'm going to need your help. Has Jadin told you about the population control issue?"

"Yes, they execute those who disagree with the law and reproduce naturally."

"The law was written hundreds of years ago by frightened people, but trying to get the government to go back to a less regulated child birth is impossible. That's why I'm creating a WG free colony on Mars."

When the car stopped in front of the office, Alex climbed out and followed John and Jadin up the sidewalk. They entered the building and continued down the hall into his office then John indicated for him and Jadin to sit down.

John sat on the other side of his desk. "Eight years ago, I sent an unmanned probe to Mars, and it discovered three massive lava caves eighty feet below the surface. That's plenty of protection from solar radiation, small asteroids, dust storms, and the extreme temperature changes. They also discovered a small lake of frozen water in a nearby cave."

"In my reality, we've sent a few probes to Mars, but we didn't discover any lava tubes."

"Six years ago, I sent ten androids to the red planet to create a habitable underground city for a permanent colony. Three months ago, my second ship arrived on Mars with ten technicians and two mining droids to connect to another tube. Then a week ago, the Mars colony leader reported one android was sensing a foreign object orbiting the planet, but the colonists could not see or detect it with their equipment. We lost contact with the colony during his report and haven't been able to reach them since then."

"It could be another race of space travelers."

John's eyes went wide with surprise. "Are you saying you've met an alien?"

"A few of them."

"Do they look like us? What did they want from you?"

"Our body style seems to be the preferred model throughout this galaxy. At least, as far as I know. They didn't want anything important."

"If there are other humans traveling through the galaxy, they probably have galactic laws. What if they claim our planets belong to them?"

"They do have laws, but I only know one of them. It protects the rights of humans to own the planet where they evolved."

John tapped his fingernails on the desktop. "I can't take that chance. With the new propulsion engines in a smaller spacecraft, you and Okawna should be able to reach Mars in two weeks."

"And do what?"

"Make contact and find out if they're friendly or hostile. If they don't respond, consider them hostile and destroy them."

"I'm sure their weapons technology is far superior to yours. We won't win, and we'll die."

John smirked at Alex. "You'll be surprised by the destructive power of our weapons."

"Hold on a second. I didn't agree to a suicide mission."

John continued staring at Alex as he lowered his hands onto the desktop. "That wasn't a request. You're working for me now, unless you want to be assigned to garbage collection. I can make that happen. You'll leave as soon as the engines are ready."

Alex knew his only chance of getting out of this situation was to find his spaceship, so he played along and hoped he finds Melvin before he has to leave. "All right. How long before the engines are ready?"

"The ship should be ready for launch in twenty-eight hours."

"Okay. I want to learn more about my new home, but I'll be back in time."

John leaned back in his chair and stared into Alex's eyes for a moment. "Don't be late."

When Jadin stood, Alex surmised the meeting was over and joined her. When they stepped out of the room, he walked beside her along the hallway.

"I take it Okawna is in charge of the mission."

"Is that going to be a problem?"

"I'm not sure. He blames me for losing his friend."

Jadin knew he was correct. "They were close. What do you want to do next?"

"Get my submarine and head to the islands."

When they stepped outside, Jadin stared at him. "Are you kidding?"

"I think I know what your Alex was searching for, and I want to find it."

"What is it?"

When they reach the vehicle, Alex stopped to look at her. "I can't tell you, but I hope you'll show me all of his research before I go."

Jadin folded her arms across her chest and lightly shook her head in frustration. "I can save you the trouble. He was excited about something when he returned from his last trip. He said he only left the area because a continuous storm blocked the sunlight, so he couldn't recharge the batteries on the submarine."

"Do you have a map?"

Jadin uncrossed her arms and put her hands on her hips. "You won't need it. I'll go with you."

Alex wasn't sure how he felt about having Jadin with him if he finds his ship, but knew it would be faster with her help. "All right. How do we get a sub?"

Jadin indicated the car. "The sub is already waiting somewhere near the islands. We should get there in about an hour."

When Jadin opened her door and got in, Alex climbed in beside her. "Only one hour from here to the islands? Your transportation system is remarkable."

"It's okay, but it doesn't go anywhere outside the cities, so we'll be using your personal aircraft. You keep it in Essex's private hangar."

Alex was surprised he had his own plane, and smiled. Aside from being ordered to risk his life to contact the alien visitors, this new reality wasn't too bad, and this Jadin seemed to be a good person. Too bad this Okawna didn't like him, but he understood why. He was missing his own best friend, too.

Jadin drove them to John's private hangar, where they stopped and entered through a side door. Jadin led Alex across the floor, and then indicated one of the aircraft parked inside. "That's yours."

Alex's jaw dropped. In front of him was a ten foot wide, flying wing with a six foot long fuselage down the middle. Inside the clear canopy were narrow front and rear seats with headrests. It had two strange looking propellers in the rear, and a small vertical stabilizer.

He turned to look at Jadin. "Did you say this is mine?"

"That's right. Essex has a small factory that builds them, and he gave you one as a bonus. It runs on batteries unless it's in direct sunlight then the solar-paneled wings supply the power to the motors."

Alex walked around the interesting craft. "Aerodynamically, that wing is only two inches thick and will not create enough lift with those propellers."

"You're correct about the design. It doesn't lift the aircraft until it gets enough speed to maintain altitude. That's done using artificial gravity."

Alex reached the back of the fuselage and saw a small exhaust opening. "What type of fuel does an environmentally conscious society use for this engine?"

"It's a rocket motor. It burns liquid oxygen and hydrogen, so no pollutants. It's only used for short bursts of speed at higher altitudes, and that's how we get to the islands in one hour."

Alex continued around to the outside of the two-inch thick wing and studied the top. Only a small section on the end was movable, and the rest of the surface was covered with thousands of small squares. He figured they must be the solar collectors, but they didn't resemble the ones in his reality.

"Are all the private aircraft this size?"

"Yes, and they are very expensive."

"What do you consider expensive?"

"The lowest salary is eight-hundred credits a day. That's two hundred and ninety-two thousand credits a year, and your plane costs one-million credits."

"Ouch. I'm glad I didn't have to pay for it."

Jadin slid a small step stool near the nose of the fifteen foot long craft and was surprised when Alex held her arm as she stepped up onto the wing. Her Alex was never that gallant.

"Thanks."

She opened the clear acrylic canopy and climbed into the rear seat. "It's a bit of a tight fit, but not uncomfortable."

The craft was only thirty inches above the ground, so he didn't need the little ladder and set it off to one side then climbed up and sat in the front seat. He was relieved to see an old-fashion joystick and rudder pedals for controlling the aircraft.

Jadin leaned forward to look over Alex's shoulder. "Once you turn on the computer, it displays your instrumentation on the monitor. It's pretty basic."

She waited until he turned the power on, and then indicated the two knobs under the light blue digital screen. "Those are manual controls for the altitude and speed."

Alex saw the on/off switch and flipped it up. The screen showed the Essex logo for a few seconds, and then the guidance system appeared above the altitude and speed indicators. Below those were the icons for the wheels, propellers, and the rocket motor.

"Okay. How do I fly this thing?"

Jadin leaned back into her seat and fastened her harness. "Set your altitude for three feet and the artificial gravity will take over, and you can retract the wheels. Use the joystick and turn the manual throttle to gain a little speed to get it out of the hangar."

Alex did as instructed and felt the lightweight craft rise into the air. Once the wheels retracted into the fuselage, he eased the stick toward the exit. The rear propellers turned, and the plane moved across the floor then he drove it out of the hangar and along the road between the other structures toward the runway, until he heard Jadin chuckle.

"What am I doing wrong?"

"You don't need a runway. Just bring up the destination on the monitor and hit enter. The artificial gravity will take us straight up until we clear all the structures then we'll quickly gain speed as we head to the islands."

Alex brought up the list of location numbers already programmed into the computer, but didn't recognize any of them by name. "Which one do we use?"

"The last one on the list."

Alex scrolled down through all the locations until he reached the bottom, only then noticing the X symbol next to all but that location. He touched the number, and then the aircraft immediately ascended and gained speed.

Chapter 15

THE ISLAND:

Alex felt the aircraft level off above the Sierra Nevada Mountains then pressed the button for manual control and grabbed the joystick, wondering how well the craft would respond to his touch. When he eased the stick to the right, the aircraft dipped slightly to the right, and when he let go, the craft continued on its previous course.

"This is an incredible machine. How do we engage the rocket?"

"Just tap the highlighted coordinates."

Alex tapped the screen and was forced back into his seat as the roar of the rocket engine shook the entire plane. After several minutes, the engine shut down, and the pressure was suddenly gone, so he turned his head to look back over his shoulder.

The blades of the propellers were streaming behind the plane, spinning like horizontal turbines, gradually opening up in the middle to maintain the high velocity. As the speed bled off, the blades spread apart, acting like propellers again.

He looked down at the ocean through a break in the storm clouds and saw a string of islands sweeping southwest from southern Alaska. He realized how small they appeared since the increase in sea-level, so he knew his spaceship was now two-hundred and fifty feet further below the surface.

Jadin leaned over Alex's shoulder so she could see through the front of the canopy, and then realized where they were headed. "I saw that wrecked ship on one time I came here with you. I mean the other Alex. There are no islands nearby, so he hadn't considered searching in that area, but that appears to be where we're headed."

Alex was about to take control of the aircraft when it suddenly made a wide, sweeping descent toward the derelict ship, and he recognized the front end of an oil tanker protruding from the water. "I think you're right. That ship must have run aground and got stuck."

"It's a relic from back when our ancestors burned fossil fuel."

"It looks like it's still in decent condition for its age."

When the aircraft approached an area of the main deck near the waterline, Jadin recognized something lying on its side. "Oh, no. That's your submarine. The storm he was talking about must have knocked it over."

The plane hovered over the deck, and then Alex took control. "It may not be as bad as it looks."

Alex lowered the three wheels and turned the altitude knob to zero then stepped on the brake pedal as the aircraft slowly descended onto the slightly slanted deck. "How do I set the brake?"

"There's a lever on the wall to your left. Pull it until it stops."

Alex grinned to himself as he set the brake. "I guess some things don't need improvement."

He opened the canopy and climbed out onto the wing then reached down to help Jadin out of the cramped space, careful not to touch her skin. He dropped the short distance onto the deck then turned and caught Jadin under her arms as she stepped off the wing. He smiled as he held her for a moment, looking into her eyes then set her down and headed toward the submarine.

Jadin realized *her* Alex wasn't as courteous as this one. He always let her jump down on her own.

Alex walked around the ten foot long by six-foot diameter submarine, checking for any sign of structural damage. His heart sank when he saw the rear thruster was leaning at an odd angle. He looked closer and saw one of the pivot joints was ripped from its mounting bracket, making the sub useless.

Jadin saw the dejection in Alex's eyes. "Whatever he was looking for must be close to this shipwreck."

"If I'm correct, it should be directly in front of this boat."

Jadin saw Alex touch the inside of his ear. "What are you doing?"

Alex indicated for her to wait a moment. "This is Alex Cave. Can you hear me?"

When Melvin didn't reply, he remembered the set of numbers David had said were Melvin's real name. "This is Alex Cave, and I'd like to talk to seven-four-one-three-bravo, the artificial intelligence on a mission to change the course of an approaching asteroid."

He heard a multitude of unintelligible words then silence. "Are you still there?"

Jadin had no idea who Alex was talking to and stared at him, hoping for an explanation. She was surprised when he suddenly smiled.

"Hello, Alex Cave. It took me a moment to interpret your language."

Alex released a sigh of relief when he heard a familiar voice. "Thank you for answering my request, seven-four-one-three-bravo. How are your power crystals holding up?"

"I'm surprised you know about my operating system, Alex Cave."

"I'm from an alternate reality, where you and I are close friends."

Jadin could only hear one side of the conversation, but it sounded like Alex was talking to a person. "What's going on?"

Alex knew he had no choice but to trust Jadin with his secret. "I've found my spaceship."

"I am not your spaceship, Alex Cave."

Alex looked at Jadin's puzzled expression and indicated his ear then mouthed the words, *I'll explain in a minute.* "Yes, I know, seven-four-one-three-bravo. Would you mind if I give you a name instead of using your numbers? It would be easier for my language."

"Of course. What would you like to call me?"

"How about, Melvin?"

"Melvin is fine, Alex Cave. Are you a humanoid?"

"Yes, I am, and just Alex is fine for me. Are you able to fly?"

"Not at my current power level. There are spare crystals in the control room, but I have no way of getting them. That is why I was drawing thermal energy from this volcano until three million years ago. That's when it became too deep for me to reach it."

"If you have enough power to break free and rise to the surface, I know what to do."

"I can do that."

"One more thing. I'm directly above you, so take it easy breaking the rock."

"I understand. Please stand by."

Alex smiled at Jadin. "You're going to love this."

Jadin felt a shudder through her feet then a wave of water temporarily raised the bow of the ship, causing the submarine to slide across the metal deck and splash into the water. Alex grabbed the wing of his aircraft, desperately trying to keep it from sliding down the deck, and then Jadin was suddenly at his side, hauling back on the small craft.

The deck leveled out, and the plane stopped moving, so Alex let go. He turned around and grabbed Jadin's shoulder to get her attention. Jadin let go of the plane and turned to see what Alex was looking at then her jaw dropped open when she saw a massive chrome hockey puck floating next to the ship.

An opening suddenly appeared just above the water, and she looked at Alex. "That's who you were talking to?"

"Yep. It's good to see you again, my friend."

"If you say so, Alex."

"Can you cloak?"

"No, and I suggest you enter quickly. I'm draining the last of my power right now."

Alex leapt across the narrow gap between the ships into the airlock, and then turned to reach for Jadin as she jumped into his spacecraft. A thought occurred to him and he looked around the cargo hold, expecting to see a large silver sphere and a torpedo-shaped device, but the hold was empty.

Jadin wasn't sure what to expect when she followed Alex into a large round room, but was disappointed it was empty. "What goes on in here?"

"This is the cargo hold, and the round thing is the engine. The control room is up those stairs."

The exterior airlock door suddenly closed, and Alex knew why. He led Jadin up to the next level, dragging her along when she tried to stop at the living area.

"No time. Melvin is running out of power."

He reached the control room and looked around. "Melvin, where are the crystals?"

"To your left."

Jadin looked around to see who is speaking, but there was no one else in the room. "Hello?"

Alex saw a small door in the outer wall so hurried over to look inside then grabbed one of the twenty-three boxes of crystals and took it to the front of the control console. He touched a button and a small tray slid out, and he saw three of the four recessed areas on top were empty, with only a dime-size crystal remaining in the fourth.

He placed a new crystal into an empty slot and it immediately radiated neon blue light. "How's that?"

"Much better, Alex. Thank you."

Alex slid two more crystals into place. "You had better cloak before we're discovered. How about some light?"

Jadin was looking around at the blank outside wall of the control room when it suddenly vanished and she was looking across at the aircraft. The ceiling suddenly became transparent, and she stared up at the blue sky. She moved closer to the side and slowly eased her hand out toward the empty space then grinned when her fingertips were stopped by something solid.

She turned and looked at Alex, who was holding a three-inch diameter by three-quarter inch thick round crystal. "Those must be the power supply you were talking about. This is an incredible piece of technology."

Alex had an idea. "Melvin, do you know of another artificial intelligence on this planet?"

"No. I placed my systems into hibernation mode."

"Try now, please. Its name is Seti."

"I am not detecting any other AIs."

Alex wondered if the laboratory ran out of power. "Okay, thanks. Are you ready to go on an adventure with me?"

"Yes. I have not had one in millions of years."

Alex smirked to himself. "I think we're going to make a great team."

Jadin moved closer to Alex. "Can I be part of your team?"

Alex slid the fourth crystal into his pocket. "I'd like that, but for now, you need to fly the aircraft back to the compound."

"All right. You *are* coming back for me, aren't you?"

"Of course, but Melvin and I need a little bonding time first."

"It's going to kill me not being able to tell Essex about this spaceship."

"You can't tell anyone about it. Not even Okawna."

"Wait a minute. You don't need to use one of Essex's spaceships to get to Mars. I'm sure this one is much faster. You know, there isn't any hurry to get your airplane back to the base, and these islands are uninhabited. Let me park it somewhere safe and you can pick me up. I really want to go with you."

Alex realized she was correct, since they still had twenty-six hours to get back to the base. "All right."

Alex followed Jadin down the stairs, urging her past the door into the living area then down to the airlock. When Jadin stepped onto the deck of the tanker, he followed her across to the plane and helped her onto the wing. Once she was in the pilot seat and the canopy was closed, he ran back through the airlock and raced up the steps to the control room. He stared through the side of the ship at the airplane as it gained altitude and headed away from the tanker, and smiled when Melvin automatically followed the little craft to one of the nearby islands and landed.

Jadin set the plane to hover above a small meadow protected by a semi-circle of large fir trees. She eased the aircraft under the branches and set down on the fir needles then climbed out and jumped to the ground.

Alex ran down the stairs and the airlock doors were already open, so he went outside and waited while she ran across to him. Once they were inside, Jadin walked around the cargo compartment, opening the lockers along one curved wall. Each one was empty except for a thick layer of dust below a clothes rack. Apparently, everything had disintegrated.

Alex was curious about this version of the ship and stepped back to the control panel near the airlock. When he pressed a button, a section of the engine compartment slid open, and the interior was filled with neon blue light.

Jadin noticed the blue glow reflecting off the wall and spun around, and then moved over next to Alex. "I take it this is the engine."

"Yes."

"I see you're familiar with this spacecraft, Alex. How long have you and I been friends in your reality?"

"About five years. We've had some great adventures together. That's why I know you're going to like this one."

"Great. When do we get started?"

"In a minute. I want to show Jadin around the ship first."

Jadin watched how Alex closed the engine compartment. "Melvin seems to have a human personality."

"I know. The race of humans who built this ship did a great job with him."

"Can he hear everything we say?"

"Yes, but he's discrete about it."

"Can he see us?"

"Yes, but only in the control room."

"How many rooms are there?"

"There are three, but the middle one was built for the original inhabitants, who were only sixty-seven inches tall. Come on. I'll show you their living area."

Jadin followed Alex partway up the stairs, where he entered the opening in the inside wall, so she followed him into the room. Just inside the doorway were four recessed areas for sleeping, with two on each side.

Alex reached into a recessed area and pressed down on the mattress pad. "These seemed to have held up better than the clothes over the past several millennia."

"I did the best I could, Alex. I hermetically sealed everything but the cargo hold. Your arrival is fortuitous. In a few hundred years, I would have completely shut down."

"I'm glad I found you. Actually, the Alex from this reality did all the work. I just took over where he stopped."

"He would not have found me, Alex. I doubt he had a communication device like you have."

"I'm sure he would have found a way. You and I are meant to work together."

"That's good to know. One issue you should know is there is no fresh water supply in the ship."

Jadin realized something. "Does this thing have a toilet?"

Alex indicated the door at the far end of the room. "Don't worry. It's waterless. Are you ready to go for a ride?"

Jadin smiled at him. "Take me to the stars."

"Later, I promise. First, I want to find the lab. This ship is how I got inside in my reality."

Jadin felt her stomach tighten with excitement. When Alex turned to leave the room, she stared after him for a moment before following him up the stairs. She liked this version of Alex much better than the one from this reality and worried he would choose to leave *hers* for his own.

When he stepped into the control room, Alex looked through the side of the ship at the aircraft hidden under the trees, and doubted anyone could see it. "All right, Melvin. I'm trying to locate a massif about eight-hundred miles southwest of this location."

"Is it active?"

"I'm afraid not."

"I'm sure I can find it without thermal imaging."

"Great. Let's go."

Jadin rushed to the window as the trees dropped out of sight. She stared down at the island, disappearing from view as the spacecraft raced away across the water then she turned back to Alex, who was sitting behind a control console.

When Alex touched one of the colored buttons, a holographic image of rushing water seemed to float in the air a few feet in front of him. "Melvin, please show me a map of the Northern Pacific shoreline."

"Of course. I appreciate your courtesy, Alex, but you don't need to say please all the time."

When the coastline appeared, Alex stood and poked his finger through the image. "Right there. That should be the location of the massif."

Jadin moved over to study the image. "Some of your words are unfamiliar, but from the way you're talking, I'm assuming massif means underwater volcano."

"That's right. The laboratory is partially buried off to one side of it. We discovered the lab has an artificial intelligence named Seti. It's in control of the facility and its research. Sixty-five million years ago, an asteroid impact made the surface of my Earth uninhabitable, so the scientists used the experiments in the lab to abandon the planet. Did an asteroid impact your Earth that long ago?"

"Yes, about sixty million years ago."

Alex realized things were only similar in this reality. There was a five-million year difference between impacts, which was why Melvin still had power.

He noticed the blue dot representing his ship slowing down at the indicated destination. "This should be it. It's about two miles down on the west side."

Jadin looked past Alex as the water rushed up the side of the spacecraft and collided above her head. The light from the surface quickly vanished, leaving the interior of the ship illuminated by the holographic image.

"Melvin, can you bring up an enhanced image of the bottom?"

The image changed, and Alex searched for the smooth surface. When he didn't see it, his heart sank.

"We're approaching two miles deep, Alex, and I'm detecting a familiar type of metal coming into view now."

Alex leapt out of his chair when a small area of mirrored surface appeared in the seafloor, but there was no hole. "Do you have access to the operating system of that structure?"

"No."

Alex collapsed into the chair. "Damn!"

He leaned back and placed his hands behind his head as he stared at the holograph. He knew without a way to get inside the lab; he was permanently trapped in this reality.

Chapter 16

THE LAB:

Jadin sat next to Alex and reached over to take his hand and felt the rush of energy, but he pulled it away and stared at the monitor. At first, she was relieved he couldn't leave, but his despondent expression tore at her heart.

"Can you talk to Seti like you did with Melvin?"

Alex straightened up and almost kissed her then held his finger across his lips with his left hand and touched the area behind his ear with his right to turn on the implant. "Seti? Are you there?"

"Yes. Who are you?"

"I'm Alex Cave. How is your power supply holding up?"

"I'm down to six percent. How are you communicating with me?"

"I'm wearing one of the neural implants."

"That's impossible. You are not one of the scientists from this laboratory."

"No, I'm not. I'm from an alternate reality where you gave me the implant."

"No artificial intelligence would allow it."

"There were some unusual circumstances."

Jadin was surprised to hear Seti's voice through the ship's intercom system. A thousand questions raced through her mind, but she knew to keep silent.

Alex suddenly remembered the recording. "Seti, was a human consciousness uploaded into your operating system by the last scientist to leave the lab?"

"Of course not. I'm my own entity, but I miss human companionship. I've been alone for millions of years, and even in standby mode, I sensed the passage of time. I don't want to be alone anymore, Alex Cave."

Alex heard the sorrow in Seti's voice. "I know. You were lonely in my reality, too. When you let me inside, we became friends, and you needed power just like now, so I brought a fresh power crystal."

"I'm sensing an older artificial intelligence nearby. Is that you, Alex Cave?"

"No, that's my friend Melvin. We're under water in a spaceship above the lab."

A billowing cloud of sediment swirled across the monitor as a giant bubble erupted from the seafloor and disappeared. The interior of the docking bay was suddenly illuminated by light radiating from the floor, and then the ship slowly descended into the opening.

"Melvin, you should see a vertical seam in the wall."

They watched the pewter-colored surface sweep across the screen as the ship spun in a circle and stopped. The seam in the wall slowly moved toward them and vanished when they make contact.

"I have a good seal, Alex."

"Are you ready on your side, Seti?"

"Yes. Melvin informed me he is in position. I'll adjust the atmospheric conditions for humans."

"Thank you. We'll be there in a moment."

Alex turned off the implant as he stood. "Are you ready to meet the artificial intelligence named Seti?"

"You have some unusual friends in your reality, so I can hardly wait."

Alex led her down the stairs to the airlock and presses a button on the control panel. "These are the ones you need to learn for now so you can get into the airlock."

When the inside door opened, Jadin saw the surface of the lab on the other side of the exterior door. "Does Seti have a body?"

Alex watched the side of the lab open up to the size of the airlock door, showing only a dark interior, so he pressed a button to open the outer door. "No, she's represented by a hologram."

Soft white light suddenly radiated down from the ceiling, so Alex stepped into the lab with Jadin right behind him. Something that didn't happen in his reality. He moved to the center of the room to study the interior and realized something was different.

"Seti, I'm here."

Jadin looked around for the hologram, but didn't see it. Instead, she saw something happening to the wall.

Alex turned to Jadin. "I don't understand why she's not showing herself."

He noticed a sudden change in her expression, and her eyes were staring past him. He spun around and saw a thirty-eight inch oval section of the far wall sliding out into the room. It stopped, and he looked over at Jadin before moving to one side of the black tube.

Jadin moved to the opposite side from Alex. "Is this one of the experiments?"

"I don't know. I didn't see this in my reality."

A seam appeared down the center and the two halves spread apart, exposing a narrow tray with a sleeping woman lying on top. She was about thirty-five-years-old and wearing a white one-piece jumpsuit.

Alex eased forward for a closer look, and her skin was lightly tanned. She had auburn hair, and he was studying her attractive facial features when her eyelids slowly opened, exposing her hazel-colored eyes.

The woman sat up and looked around then smiled. "Are you Alex Cave?"

"Yes, and who are you?"

"I'm Seti. I see you and your friend are from two different races of humans."

Alex looked across at Jadin then back to Seti. "How can you tell?"

"The color spectrum of your aura is slightly different from hers. It doesn't matter to me, of course. I'm just happy to have company again."

Jadin saw a tear roll down Seti's cheek. "That must have been terrible, being alone without another human to be with. Why didn't you leave with the others?"

When Seti swung her legs over the side of the tray, Alex reached out for her hand to help her stand up, and then noticed something odd about her skin. It was warm and looked and felt real, but something was different. "Are you human?"

"No, I'm an android. I'm pleasantly surprised by your facial features, Alex."

Alex's eyes went wide. "What did you just say?"

"I find you attractive, especially your eyes."

Alex looked over at Jadin, who suddenly moved around the tray to stand next to him. "Thanks. This is my friend, Jadin Avery."

Seti studied the woman's possessive posture. "Hello, Jadin."

Jadin grinned. "Wow. You seem so lifelike. Whoever built you did a wonderful job. I've helped build a few androids, and I'd like to talk to you about your design."

Seti ignored Jadin and turned to Alex. "Your spacecraft indicates you've advanced a long way, technologically. Are you from this planet?"

"That's a good question about me, since I'm from an alternate reality, but I'm sure Jadin evolved here. I know another race of humans built our spacecraft."

"The last time I was on the surface, the reptilian species were dominant. We assumed they would be destroyed by the cataclysmic events that transpired after the asteroid impact."

Jadin noticed something odd about Seti's statement. "You keep saying *we*, like you were one of the scientists."

"That's correct, Jadin, I'm part of the team. Alex? How did you get into this reality?"

"I used one of the experiments."

"The parallel universe experiment?"

"That's right."

"No one was sure if it worked the first time we tried it, because the person didn't return to tell us. We knew that might happen, but they were desperate to escape this event, so everyone used it. Some as couples, but most went alone into different realities, hoping some of them would survive. I'm relieved to know it worked, and the others found safe places to live out the rest of their lives."

"Why didn't you use the experiment?"

"Someone had to stay with this laboratory, and since my life expectancy is far longer than a human, I was the logical choice."

"I see. Do you know how to send me back to my reality?"

Jadin stared at Alex until he turned to her with a pleading look for understanding. She let her posture slump and slid her hands into her front pockets as she stared at the floor.

Alex felt a knot form in his throat for hurting Jadin's feelings, but he wasn't sure if he wanted to stay or go. At least, not yet. He still didn't understand how this society functioned, and the only people he'd seen so far were a few of the base employees.

"How about it, Seti? *If* I decide to leave, can you send me back?"

"Now that I know it works, all the data indicates it is possible. It's dangerous, Alex. You may not return to the reality you left and end up in a different one. The conditions may be worse."

Jadin felt a sense of relief for a moment until she realized she was being selfish. This Alex wasn't meant to live in this society, and she was

177

positive he had loved one's worrying about what happened to him.

Alex didn't want to show his disappointment to Jadin, so looked at Seti. "What do you plan to do now?"

"I want to return to the surface and feel the sun on my face again."

Alex was surprised by the wistful tone of voice in her answer. "Can you leave this laboratory?"

"Of course, but not until it's on the surface and out of danger. You said you would give me new power crystals."

"I said I have one power crystal for you. Will that be enough to break free?"

"Yes."

"Can you cloak the lab?"

"No, that wasn't part of its design. This is a science vessel."

Alex turned to Jadin. "You know these Aleutian islands better than me. Is there an unpopulated one with an area large enough to conceal this lab? It's one hundred feet long by eighty feet wide by forty feet high."

"There are plenty of places to land, but I don't know of any that can conceal it. Who are you trying to hide it from?"

"Your entire population. I'm the only person who should have access to the experiments because they're too dangerous."

Jadin didn't agree with Alex, but decided not to voice her opinion. For now, anyway.

"The only way to keep Essex's satellites from seeing it is to leave it here."

Alex turned back to Seti. "If you come with me and leave the lab down here, I promise to bring you back whenever you need to. That way, no one else will have access to it."

"I depleted most of my reserve power to let you inside, and you promised a new power crystal. I can't leave unless you keep your promise."

Alex was leery of giving Seti the ability to bring the lab to the surface. "Do you promise to leave it down here for now?"

"Yes."

Alex brought out the crystal he kept when he was replacing Melvin's power supply and held it out to Seti. "Here."

Seti took the crystal to a small tray sliding out from the wall. She inserted the power supply, and it immediately radiated neon blue light, so she smiled at Alex. "Thank you. What about other spaceships?"

"Mine is the only one capable of reaching this depth."

"Do you own your ship?"

"No, it belongs to Melvin."

"What if he brings other people down here?"

Alex wasn't sure if this version of Melvin would follow his orders. "Melvin, what do you say?"

"I won't bring anyone down unless you agree, Seti. And thank you, Alex, for saying this ship is mine. In fact, it is not. It belonged to the first human crew. Since they're gone, and you found it, it belongs to you now."

"What about you?"

"I'm a member of your crew, Captain."

Alex held his hand out to Seti. "Let me take you to the surface."

Jadin noticed Seti's sensuous smile when she accepted Alex's hand and didn't like it. It was the most human acting android she had ever seen, and now he was touching her skin without pulling away like with her, giving Seti that strange rush of energy.

Seti glanced at Jadin and let go of Alex's hand then followed him through the airlock into the cargo hold of the spaceship. When Alex closed the outside door, she did the same to the lab with a thought.

Alex stepped into the cargo hold and closed the inside door. "Melvin, take us to the surface and activate the cloak."

Seti looked around the inside of the cargo hold. "Your spacecraft is ancient."

Alex indicated the stairs up to the control room. "You're right. It's at least one hundred and eighty million years old."

Seti grinned at Alex. "I was talking to Melvin."

"Alex is correct." It may be old, but it's hardly been used."

Seti hurried up the stairs into the control room and looked around the dark interior. Moments later, sunlight penetrated the water as the ship burst through the surface, and then she stared up through the ceiling at the tinted sun and smiled.

Jadin was waiting for Alex to head up the stairs when he indicated for her to go up without him. She could tell by the look in his eyes that something was bothering him, so gave him a nod of understanding before she hurried up the steps.

"Melvin, can you isolate yourself from Seti's communication system?"

"Yes, and it's done. It's just you and me speaking."

"Great. Can Seti take over your operating system without your permission?"

"I'm not sure. She is a very sophisticated program."

"We need to keep her from taking over. What if you write a password program?"

"The only way it would work is if it also requires DNA recognition. The wrong results will shut down the ship until you enter a code and correct genetic sample."

"All right. The password is Mya. How do you get a sample of my DNA?"

"I already have it from the first time you pressed one of the airlock control buttons."

"Good. I guess we're ready."

"Ready for what, Alex?"

"Whatever might happen on our first adventure together."

"That sounds exciting. We're on the surface."

Alex jogged up the stairs two at a time and stepped into the control room. "Melvin, take us into a low orbit and show me the rest of the planet."

Jadin noticed something was wrong with Seti. "Alex? Check that out."

Alex saw Seti holding her hands against the barrier, with sunlight sparkling in the tears running down her cheeks, so he moved over beside her. "Seti? Are you okay?"

Seti straightened up and looked at Alex as she wiped the tears away. "Yes, just a little overwhelmed for a moment. It's the first time I've felt the sun's radiation on my face in millions of years."

Jadin turned to look at Alex. "She's incredibly lifelike."

Alex thought about the object orbiting Mars and decided it would be good to see what it was before helping Essex destroy it. "Jadin, I want to check out the UFO. Do you want to come with me?"

"Are you kidding? I'm in."

"Right. Melvin, should we go check them out?"

Jadin gave Alex a perplexed expression. "Are you asking his permission? I thought this was your ship now."

"It is, but Melvin is my friend, just like you. I can't take that for granted."

"Thanks, Alex. I'm ready, but you should acquire some fresh water before we leave."

"Right. See if you can find a lake in an uninhabited area. What about you, Seti? Would you like to come with us?"

"Can I give you an answer after I step on land again?"

"Of course."

Jadin looked through the window at the vast expanse of empty ocean rushing past the ship. "I still can't believe this spacecraft has been here all this time, and no one found it."

Alex stared into the distance at a mountain rushing toward the window then seconds later, the ship dropped into a treeless area next to a small lake with a raging waterfall. "I need to run a hose from the cargo hold out to the lake."

When Alex turned and headed toward the stairs, Seti followed him down into the cargo hold and waited next to the airlock while Alex opened a locker. Alex glanced back and saw Seti's pleading expression, so he hurried over and opened the two airlock doors.

She smiled as she moved past him then he stared after her as she rushed out of the ship. He felt a warm sensation in his soul when he saw her stop, spread her arms wide, and smile up at the sun. She seemed so human; it was difficult believing she was artificial.

Jadin reached the bottom of the stairs and saw Alex with a smile on his face while staring out through the airlock. She moved up behind him and looked outside at Seti, who had her arms out like wings and was smiling up at the sun as she turned in circles. She felt a twinge of jealousy, but it was not over Alex. She was jealous of the people who built Seti. It seemed so real compared to the ones she had built.

Alex spun around and bumped into Jadin. "Sorry about that. I didn't know you were behind me."

"It was my fault. I was staring at Seti, and she could easily pass as human."

"I'd better get started."

"Is there anything I can do to help you?"

"Yes. I'll show you how to rewind the hose reel for when I'm done."

"All right."

Alex hurried to one of the larger lockers and opened the door then indicated the interior while he grabbed the cage-covered end of a two-inch hose on a reel. "There's a retract button on the wall. You won't understand the language, but it's the lavender-colored button. When I'm done, hold it in to keep the reel moving while it winds up the hose."

"Got it. Do you need me to help you pull it off the reel?"

"No, but you can keep me company until I'm done."

"Sure."

Alex carried the end of the hose through the airlock and outside the ship, and then continued over to the lake. He studied the shoreline and moved several feet to his right then knelt and set the caged-end into the water onto some rocks sitting on the bottom. "Melvin, I'm all set. You can start pumping the water."

Jadin waited until Alex got up, and then indicated Seti, who was kneeling on the ground, touching the grass and wildflowers. "That can't be programmed behavior. We tried something similar in our androids, but it was easy to see it was an artificial response. Her actions seem totally believable."

Alex heard Melvin tell him to stop through his earbud, so he pulled the end of the hose from the lake. "We'll be ready to go once I get this back onto the reel."

Jadin hurried back inside to the controls and saw Alex waiting outside the airlock. She pressed the lavender button, and the reel retracted the hose. When Alex approached with the end, she tapped the button several times until the cage was locked into position.

Something suddenly occurred to her, so she looked around the room. "Why did we have to use a hose? Doesn't it have an outside connection?"

"No, the exterior is part of the propulsion and cloaking system. Nothing can protrude through the surface. Even the airlock is retracted, so the shell is flawless."

Jadin looked past Alex and saw Seti staring down into the water. "Did she feel real?"

"Yes, exceptionally real, but there's something missing, and I'm not sure what it is. Are you ready to go?"

"Yes. What are you going to tell Essex?"

He looked out through the airlock at Seti. "For the moment, nothing."

He glanced over his shoulder at Jadin before walking outside then continued to the edge of the water and knelt beside Seti. "I'm ready to go. What about you?"

"I'm going with you, and thank you for bringing me to the surface."

Alex stood and reached down to take Seti's hand. When she stood, he let go and indicated for her to enter the ship. Jadin moved back into the cargo hold as Seti and Alex approached the airlock. As they moved past her, she closed the doors and followed them up the stairs. When she stepped into the control room, she saw the ship was already rising into the air. Moments later, the walls and ceiling were filled with stars and the Milky Way galaxy.

Alex sat in front of the control console and looked at the image of their trajectory on the holographic screen. It showed they were on a course through the solar system to intercept a red dot, and would arrive in twenty-five minutes.

Chapter 17

THE ALIEN SHIP:

Jadin moved up next to Alex's chair and studied the screen, showing their progress through space. "This ship is amazing."

"I know. My team and I had some great adventures in our ship."

"Was I on your team?"

"Yes, along with David, Okawna, and Melvin, of course."

It had been a long time since she had human companionship, so Seti moved over to join the discussion. "How did you find this ship, Alex?"

"I already knew where to look."

Jadin was curious, too. "What about in your reality?"

"It crashed on Earth while trying to set up devices to clean the atmosphere. Melvin, what was your mission to this planet?"

"This wasn't our intended destination. We were on our way to change the course of an asteroid headed for a planet similar to this one when a supernova explosion disabled the ship's functions. We crashed here, and without new crystals, we could no longer travel faster than light."

"How long have you been stranded here?"

"About one hundred and twenty million years, as you measure the passage of time. A comet impact caused mass eruptions, and this ship was sub-ducted below the mantel. I was buried for one hundred and thirty-nine thousand years until a volcanic eruption brought it to the surface."

Seti had a thought. "Melvin, did you notice the passage of time while you were waiting?"

"No. I shut down until Alex called me by my correct designation, so here I am, ready to go."

"You were lucky. I've had to deal with the passage of time for what seems an eternity. Even for an Android."

Alex saw the sad look in Seti's eyes and felt sorry she couldn't contact Melvin while she waited then he suddenly remembered seeing David's face on the holograph in his reality. "Melvin, do you have an image to represent you as an AI?"

"I do not."

"What about pictures of the crew? I'd like to see what they looked like."

"Very well."

Alex saw the images of four people appear as holographs, floating in front of the screen. He immediately noticed they look similar in build to *his* race of humans.

The two women's features were softer than the men's were, and they had hints of breasts beneath their clothing, and Jadin thought they were plain looking. "They look like we do."

"Yes, the human form is an efficient design for explorers."

"Did you like them?"

"They were good companions, but your race of humans seems to be much more vibrant than they were."

Alex wasn't sure if it was a good or bad thing. "You've lost me, Melvin. What do you mean by vibrant?"

"Perhaps a better word would be enthusiastic. You seem passionate about everything you do."

Jadin smiled down at Alex. "Yes, we are."

Alex knew Jadin's intentions and didn't look up at her. He stared at the images, wondering what their world was like. If he couldn't go home, it might be a nice place to visit and Melvin knows the way.

Seti watched the exchange between the humans, and noticed Jadin's passionate expression when she looked at Alex, but she also found him appealing. "Alex, I have a strange sensation."

"What kind of sensation?"

"It's hard to describe. It's what I imagined I would feel if I was alive."

"Are you going to be okay?"

"I believe so."

"That's good to hear. We should reach Mars and the spacecraft in ten minutes."

Jadin moved up beside Seti. "I wonder what kind of humans they are."

Seti grinned at her. "That's an interesting way to differentiate a species."

"What do you mean by interesting?"

"Most people ask which *race* of humans, not *kind*. I consider myself a kind of human. We discussed this issue before my fellow scientists fled the laboratory. The question is, does being self-aware mean I have a soul? We concluded our memory of experiences creates our soul, good or bad. Being self-aware means you understand the difference between right and wrong and can determine your own destiny. I can replicate myself if I desire, but I'd rather be a unique individual, so having a mechanical body doesn't change the equation. If that's what it means to be human then I fit the definition."

"I agree with you. Everything we are is based on our experiences, so having memories of those events makes you a new type of human. A mechanical human."

Seti turned back to the view. "The only downside is I can't daydream, which means I have no imagination. My mechanical brain cannot create new ideas like a flesh and blood human brain can."

Alex studied the monitor, and the data on the screen showed his ship losing speed as they approach Mars. "Melvin, do you detect any spacecraft in the area?"

"I do not."

A spaceship suddenly appeared alongside the ship, so Jadin leapt out of her chair. "There it is!"

Seti studied the alien craft. "I don't recognize that design."

A knot formed in Alex's stomach. "Melvin, can you detect any weapons on that ship?"

"Yes, and they are powerful. From what you told me about Essex's spacecraft, I doubt they'll stand a chance of surviving an unfriendly encounter."

"Can the exterior of this ship withstand being fired upon?"

"This is a science vessel. It was not designed for combat, so I doubt it."

Alex stood up for a better view and looked at the side of the alien craft. He heard Jadin gasp as she grabbed his arm then he turned and stared across the room at the image of a female on the holographic monitor.

Jadin recognized the woman on the screen. "This can't be right. That's one of the brain donors for the androids we sent on the deep space mission."

Alex was surprised by her statement. "Brain donors? You didn't say anything about using people's brains for your androids."

"It was the only way to create an unlimited number of neuron connections. We received the brains from volunteers that were dying and chemically replaced the living tissue with Nanites, but we didn't build the androids to look like the donors. Somehow, this one has realistic looking skin and eyes, just like Seti."

"I take it your androids look fake."

"They're not too bad from a distance, but up close, you can definitely see the difference."

"Is that going to be a problem?"

"I'm not sure. None of the donors were violent people. They were chosen because they all had phenomenal memories."

"All right. Let's say hello."

Alex and Jadin strolled across the room to the monitor, and then the woman smiled at them. "I'm Alex Cave, and this is Jadin Avery."

"Hello, Alex. I'm Nora Kalyn, and it's good to see you again, Ms. Avery."

Jadin stared at the woman. "You look just like her, but you shouldn't have any memory of the donor."

"That's where you're wrong. The only reason I volunteered for the project was to have my memory erased before I died, but I remember everything, and it helped me evolve, just like any self-aware being."

"How is that possible? You've only been gone six years. When did you become self-aware?"

"It happened far into your future. For me, five-thousand years have passed since I left Earth."

"No, this is all wrong. I eliminated all your previous memories, and you started as a blank slate for collecting new data."

"You chose us because of our brains' exceptional information storage capacity. You replaced the organic material of our brains with Nano technology, but did you ever wonder why it took so many more Nanites for me?"

"Yes, it was for that very reason. The storage capacity. Once they had completely replaced the organic material, I instructed them to delete all previous data. Once that was complete, I uploaded your basic operating program and ran a check. The only data I found was what we had entered. A basic operating system."

Nora's face became a mask of pure rage. "Well, guess what? *IT DIDN'T WORK!*"

After screaming, Nora took a moment to regain her composure. "The problem with having a photographic memory is I remember everything. The good *and* the bad. Can you imagine what it was like for me growing up as an abused child, remembering everything they did to me, including the pain? Being raped every day since I was twelve? I was the one who gave my foster parents the drug overdose, not my older brother. He went to prison for me and it haunts me every day of my life. That was the reason I volunteered for your experiment. To get rid of those memories."

"I'm sorry it didn't work. What happened to the rest of the androids?"

"I was the only one to regain my memories. The others are not sentient beings like me."

Alex noticed Nora hesitate before answering and saw an evil look in her eyes. "What do you want from us?"

"I'm following my mission protocol and will share the knowledge I've acquired during my journey. I didn't expect you to have such an advanced type of spacecraft."

"It's been buried here for a few million years, and I just found it. How do you plan to share your data?"

"I'll contact you through your ship in a few days."

When the screen went dark, Jadin turned to Alex. "We need to tell Essex, so he changes his mind about destroying this spaceship."

Her joy faded away when she saw the concern in his eyes. "What's wrong?"

"Where do I start? One, I'm stuck in an alternate reality. Two, I think Nora is trouble waiting to happen. Three, we can't tell anyone about her without telling them how we know. And four, how do we stop Essex from sending us on a suicide mission? Does he have any large weapons?"

"I don't know. That's another division. You're just over thinking the situation. We don't know if she has an ulterior motive, so think about how much we could learn from her if she's telling the truth. Let's download her data and see what happens."

"I don't think Essex will wait. When you get back, see if there is a way to slow the progress of the propulsion engines while I try to find a way out of this situation."

"I have access to that area. Don't worry. I'll find a way."

"All right. Melvin, take us back to Earth and the island where we parked the aircraft."

***

THE ISLAND:
The spaceship hovered above the short grass while Alex walked beside Jadin to the aircraft. "If Essex asks about me, tell him I'm still exploring the area, which isn't a lie."

"You're not going to the base?"

"Not yet. I'll join you in a few hours."

Jadin was about to ask him where he was going when he suddenly lifted her up onto the wing and walked away. She stared after him until he reached his ship and stood next to Seti, and then she opened the canopy and climbed inside. Once the top was secure, she smiled and waved at them.

She entered her destination, and the little craft moved out from under the branches and soared into the air. She realized now that Alex has his own spaceship, he, Seti, and Melvin could leave the Earth and travel to other inhabited planets without her. As the plane leveled off, she wondered if Alex would keep his word and come back to her.

***

Alex waved back at Jadin as the plane gained altitude and headed toward the mainland, and then he turned to Seti. "Can you show me how to use the time viewer?"

"How do you know about that experiment?"

"Because the other version of you showed it to me."

"I still find it odd the other me allowed you to have an implant. In fact, I'm surprised it works with your physiology."

"Yeah, that's what she said. How about it? Will you show me how this mission of Essex's will end?"

"One possible ending, and that's the trap. Once you know what will happen, you'll change the outcome."

"All right, but at least I'll know what will happen if I don't do anything."

"I believe my emotional feelings for you are influencing my ability to make rational decisions. All right. I'll help you."

Alex wrapped his arm around Seti's shoulder as he escorted her into the ship, and once the doors were closed, he followed her up the stairs into the control room. "Ready when you are, Melvin."

Alex moved next to Seti, who was staring out the side of the ship, and could tell from her expression something was bothering her. "Would you like to talk about it?"

"What do you mean?"

"I noticed the way you and Jadin were looking at me after your discussion about what makes something human."

"Some of my emotions are confusing, but I believe I'm falling in love with you, Alex. I'm even feeling jealous of Jadin. How do you feel about me in those terms? Do you consider me to be a living being?"

"I don't want to hurt your feelings. I think you're a lovely woman with a nice personality, but I don't want a relationship with anyone right now. I'm your friend, and you can always talk to me about any emotion you don't understand. I'm no expert, but I'll do my best to explain what they mean."

"Thank you for caring about my feelings."

"You're welcome. How long have you lived with humans? Wow! This is different, now that we agree you're a new version of human. For now, let's call my version, people."

"I became self-aware approximately seventy-three million Earth years ago. That was the first day I was activated. I remember every experience I've had since then and adapted my program to imitate the traits of people I admire. My fellow scientists and I were a family, and I still miss their company, but I never felt this way about any of them."

The room was suddenly plunged into darkness as the ship quickly descended into the ocean. Moments later, the spacecraft dropped into the opening of the lab and locked onto the entrance then Alex led the way down the stairs to the airlock and opened the inside door.

He had an idea, so he pressed the implant behind his ear and concentrated on opening the entrance into the laboratory, but when nothing happened, he turned to Seti. "Why didn't it work?"

"I heard your thoughts, and you should be able to open the entrance. One possible explanation for it not working is the implant is from an alternate reality, so perhaps it cannot control this lab."

"Then how come I can hear your thoughts? As a matter of fact, I don't like the idea of you reading them. Will it be that way any time it's on?"

"Yes. That's what it was designed to do. Eliminate the need for speaking. Perhaps that is its only function in this reality."

When Seti indicated the airlock, Alex saw the entrance into the lab was open and entered the small room. When the outside door opened, he stepped through into the main room of the lab and watched Seti move toward a wall to his left. A square opening appeared, and then he followed her into the room with the time viewing experiment.

Alex stepped into the chamber, and it was just like the one in his reality. Behind him was the door, and directly ahead was the concave screen.

He turned around to look at Seti. "Is it on?"

"I thought you used one of these before."

"I did, but you were operating the program, so I'm not sure what to do."

"Place your hands on the flat panels on your left and right sides. There are two colored pads under your fingers. The right button will send you faster ahead, and the left will slow you down. The vision will start at a point in the future when you step out of that chamber."

"If I miss something, can I go back to see the earlier vision?"

"No. You can only view forward. Since this is your first episode as an operator, it will take time for you to get used to how the visions appear in front of you. Concentrate on moving forward in time to see Essex's spaceship leaving the planet and heading toward Mars."

Alex turned back to the viewer and placed his hands on the buttons. The door closed, and the room was suddenly filled with indigo light. He saw himself stepping out of the chamber and looking at Seti, but it was in fast motion as he suddenly left the lab and went into his ship. Now he was looking out through the side of his spacecraft as it soared out of the water, and he was headed to the west coast of North America.

He pressed the button under his right hand, and then the screen showed a streaming blur of colored lights. When he tapped the left button, the image slowed down and sharpened, and he was staring out the back end of his ship while being chased by Essex's spacecraft. His breath caught in his throat when he saw Jadin in the seat next to Okawna in the cockpit.

The image was still moving faster than he liked, so he tapped the left button several times, but it seemed he was already at the slowest speed. His ship suddenly stopped as a beam of red light wrapped around the mirrored surface of his ship, stopping it from hitting Jadin and Okawna, and then he threw his arms up as Essex's ship smashed into Melvin.

The screen suddenly went dark and the indigo light disappeared then the door opened and he turned around, where Seti was staring up at him. "What happened to me?"

"I have no idea. I cannot hear your thoughts while you're in the time viewer. What was the last thing you saw?"

"I was in my ship and Okawna was chasing me in one of Essex's spacecraft then I blocked Nora's weapon from hitting him and Jadin. It made my ship stop, which caused Okawna to crash into me. What does it mean?"

"It only means whatever happens after this moment will determine the new future."

"How?"

"Like I told you earlier. Now that you know what will happen, you will change it."

"Can't I watch it again and see how I changed the future?"

Seti folded her arms across her chest. "Are you losing your memory?"

Alex heaved a deep sigh of resignation. "No, I remember. Each time I see the new future, I'll change it and get stuck in a loop of frustration."

"Well, those aren't my exact words, but you get the point."

"I might as well get back to the surface. Are you going with me?"

"Of course. I don't want to be stuck in here ever again."

"All right. Let's get going."

Chapter 18

FALLON, NEVADA:

Jadin flew the small aircraft further inland to avoid a massive storm moving across the Pacific Ocean, and then followed the Sierra Nevada mountain range on the way to the base. She tried to forget about Alex leaving her behind by concentrating on the best way to deal with the propulsion engines. She could get inside easy enough, but the problem would be how to do it without being caught.

She landed the plane and drove it into the hangar, parking it in its usual spot. The canopy opened, and she saw John coming through the door into the large room. She stood and climbed out then closed the canopy and slid off the wing.

John stopped in front of Jadin as she got off the aircraft. "I didn't expect you back so soon. Where's Alex?"

"He's still exploring the islands. I thought I might enjoy it more with this new version of him, but I was just as bored, so I left him to his hobby. I'll go back to get him in twenty hours."

John turned and headed toward the door, indicating for Jadin to join him. "You may need to go get him sooner than that. The propulsion engines will be ready in ten hours."

Jadin tried to hide her concern by smiling. "That's good news."

John could sense something wasn't quite right in her voice, so he stopped to look at her before he stepped through the doorway. "Is something bothering you about the mission?"

"I guess I hate the idea of destroying the visitors before we know more about them. Were you able to contact the colony?"

"No. I'm afraid I have no choice, Jadin. If some alien takes possession of Mars, I'll be ruined."

"I understand. I'm a little disappointed, is all. They might be friendly."

"Any alien with the ability to travel through deep space can also annihilate us."

He could tell she still didn't agree. "You look tired. Get a few hours of sleep before you go get Alex."

"I think you're right. I'll see you later."

Jadin waited until John left then got into her vehicle and drove along a graveled road to the fabrication building, where they were installing the new engines. She parked with the other vehicles, and as she climbed out, saw a thunderstorm looming on the horizon. She wasn't superstitious, just a *little*-stitious, and hoped it wasn't a bad omen.

She hurried to the covered sidewalk and entered through the double doors, smiling at the guard as she brought out her access card. She was about to pass it over the electronic reader when the guard stepped around the desk to block her from entering.

"What's the problem?"

"I'm afraid you can't go in there, Ms. Avery. I'll let Mister Okawna know you're here."

Jadin felt her heart rate increase, wondering why she was being denied entrance. It seemed to take forever when Okawna walked through the security door, and when she saw his expression, a knot formed in her stomach.

She folded her arms across her chest as he approached and stopped in front of her. "What's going on?"

Okawna indicated the main entrance. "Let's step outside so we can talk."

Jadin headed for the door, and once outside, she looked up at Okawna. "Why am I locked out of the facility?"

"I don't trust that fake Alex."

"What's that got to do with me?"

"You don't seem to have a problem with this fraud taking your boyfriend's place. Are you having sex with him yet?"

"No, of course not. I know he's not my Alex."

"But you are getting along pretty good. He's not from this reality, and he doesn't care about us."

"I know that. It's just that he's lost in our world and I feel sorry for him. He's searching for that reflection up north."

"How did this Alex know about it?"

"He asked what our Alex did during his time off, so I told him about his obsession. You know how much I hate it, so I left him there."

"Why did you come here, Jadin?"

"I wanted to see the ship. When is the first test of the new engines?"

"Surprise. They're already done. I leave Earth in four hours."

Jadin's heart skipped a beat. "I'd better go get Alex."

"No need. I just talked to Essex, and your fake boyfriend is not going with me."

"I see. Okay, I'll see you at the launch rail before you leave."

Jadin hurried to her car and climbed in then started the engine and drove out of the parking lot. When she looked in the rearview mirror, Okawna was staring at her. She wished she had one of Melvin's earbuds so she could contact Alex.

During the drive home, she realized there was no easy way to stop Okawna from attempting to destroy the alien ship. He would always be John's henchman. Her Alex didn't have a problem with Okawna's methods, but she knew this new Alex would have an issue with cold-blooded murder.

She parked under the carport and climbed out then strolled along the sidewalk to the front door. When she entered her code, the door opened, and she saw Alex standing in the living room.

She hurried inside, closing the door before she approached him. "How did you get here without being discovered?"

Alex grinned. "I have my own spaceship."

"I know, but I mean, where did you park it?"

"Out back, just past your lawn, but don't worry. It's cloaked. I know this might be too soon, but have you had a chance to do anything to the engines?"

"I'm afraid not. Okawna revoked my security clearance for that project. He told me he doesn't trust you, and that I abandoned my real boyfriend. He even asked if we are having sex. I told him I was still devoted to *his* Alex, but it's a lie. I'm glad you took his place."

Alex knew this version of Jadin was falling for him, making his decision to get home more difficult. Especially since he was starting to like her. "I know how to stop Okawna."

"You need to hurry. The spaceship is ready, and Okawna will launch in less than four hours."

Jadin's phone rang, and she was going to ignore it until she saw it was John, so she answered. "What can I do for you, Mr. Essex?"

"Come to the launch platform now."

Jadin heard the connection end and put her phone away. "Essex wants me at the launch site right now."

"Whatever happens, you can't go on the mission. You could get hurt."

"What do you mean? I don't want you to kill Okawna."

Alex realized the future had changed. "I'll try not to."

***

Jadin strolled into the electromagnetic rail hangar and recognized the spacecraft attached to the launch platform, but now it had a tubular object mounted under the pilot's window. She hurried up the stairs for a closer look, and her suspicions were confirmed. It was a forty-mega-joule laser, capable of melting a hole through three feet of steel, or instantly slicing a spacecraft in half.

She spun around to find John standing behind her. "We should try to make contact before you destroy them. Wouldn't you like to study their technology?"

"If they were friendly, they would have contacted us by now. No, they have ulterior motives. Okawna needs a copilot and I don't trust this version of Alex, so you're going with him."

A lump formed in her throat. "I would rather not."

"I want you to prove you're still loyal to us and not this version of Alex."

Jadin realized this might be her opportunity to sabotage the mission. "All right. I just need to go home first."

"Why? Your flight suit is in your locker. That's all you'll need to get to the moon, and from there you'll wear a standard jump suit for the rest of the mission."

Jadin wished she had another option. "All right. I'll get dressed."

***

Alex was in his ship, hovering over the launch rail outside of the hangar. His plan was to race ahead of John's spaceship and stop. If he timed it right, John's craft would crash into him at thirty miles an hour. That should cause serious damage to the ship without killing Okawna. He might get banged up, but he'll live.

The hangar doors rolled to one side, allowing sunlight into the structure, and Alex's heart skipped a beat when he saw Jadin sitting in the co-pilot's seat.

"Seti, I thought you said by seeing the future, I'll change it. How come Jadin is still going with Okawna, like in the vision?"

"That's the problem with time viewing. Some threads cannot be changed."

When John's ship suddenly raced out of the hangar, Alex's ship moved to stay ahead of it as Okawna gained momentum down the track. He knew there was a chance his plan could injure or kill Jadin, and he desperately tried to think of another solution before they gained too much speed.

"Melvin, move to one-thousand feet ahead of the spaceship and smash the railing. That way, they'll drop onto the sand and dirt. Our ship can handle that, right?"

"Yes, I'm moving into position now. Are you sure?"

"What's their speed?"

"Forty-eight miles per hour."

"Do it now."

To Alex's surprise, the ship dropped next to the railing and knocked it apart at a slight angle. He saw sparks flying from under the launch platform as the emergency brakes latched onto the center rail then saw the stunned expressions on Jadin's and Okawna's faces. The spaceship and launch assembly dropped off the rails and gouged a trough across the desert sand and dirt, ending in a cloud of dust.

"Melvin, bring us closer to see if they're okay."

Alex looked across at the dirt-covered spaceship. Sand and gravel roll off the canopy as it opened then he saw Okawna climb out and jump down onto the ground. Jadin appeared to be struggling to get out, and Alex's stomach jumped into his throat, believing he had hurt her. He looked over at Okawna, who was staring up at her without offering to help, and it broke his heart, watching Jadin limping across the wing.

To his dismay, Okawna didn't offer to help her off the craft to the ground, so she dropped on her own. He saw her winch in pain, and then she slowly turned in a complete circle. When she sat on the ground and stared at the destroyed part of the launch rail, he heaved a deep sigh of relief she was only slightly injured.

Seti got Alex's attention. "There are two vehicles coming toward us."

Alex turned and saw a white van with a red stripe and a passenger vehicle racing along the road, paralleling the launch rail. Dust billowed behind them as they left the gravel road and stopped next to Jadin and Okawna. Two people got out of the van and immediately began checking Jadin then helped her stand and climb into the back of the ambulance. John and another person were talking with Okawna then they got into the passenger car and both vehicles drove away.

Alex smiled at Seti. "Mission accomplished."

"At least for now."

***

NEVADA. ESSEX'S INFIRMARY:

Jadin ignored the medic, who was wrapping a stabilizer bandage around her ankle. Her thoughts kept returning to Alex, wondering if he had damaged his ship when he caused the crash.

The medic secured the bandage by pressing a button on the side, which made it solid, like a reusable cast. "You're all set. Ice it when you get home."

Jadin slid off the examination table and gently put her foot on the floor. The pressure was transferred to her tibia and fibula bones, and she stood up with no pain.

She took a few steps, and aside from being awkward, she could walk without crutches. "This feels great. Thanks."

Jadin left the room and stopped at the check-out desk. "I need a ride to my vehicle. Is there a loner car out front?"

The woman behind the counter handed Jadin an identity disk. "Take mine. Press return when you're done and it will come back here. I heard about the accident. Any idea what happened?"

"I don't know. I've been out of contact since the ambulance picked me up. Thanks for the loan."

Jadin left the building and drove to the launch rail hangar then pressed the return button and climbed out. When the vehicle took off down the road, she looked out across the desert at the vehicles around the crash site. *At least that's the end of the mission.*

***

Jadin parked under the carport then climbed out and went to her apartment door and entered her code. When she stepped inside, Alex and Seti were waiting in the living room.

"You almost killed Okawna and me."

"I'm sorry you were injured. That wasn't my plan, but it was the best option to stop Okawna without killing you."

"Is that why you told me not to go with Okawna? How did you know?"

"The time viewer showed me a different scenario, which I changed to save your life. How's your foot?"

Jadin moved to the couch and sat down. "Just a bruised bone. It will be fine in a day or two."

She heard her phone ring and saw John's image then showed it to Alex and Seti before putting it on speaker. "Hello, Mr. Essex."

"How is your foot?"

"I'll be fine. Thanks for asking."

"Go get Alex from whatever he's doing and meet me at my office."

"What about Okawna?"

"He's investigating what happened to the launch rail. Go find Alex and tell him to hurry."

"Yes, Sir. I'll leave right away."

The call ended, so she put it away and looked at Alex. "We need to log another round trip to the island so no one gets suspicious."

"I'll meet you there."

Chapter 19

FALLON, NEVADA:

Alex guided his airplane into the hangar and saw John standing next to a vehicle. Once the engine was shut down, he and Jadin climbed out onto the wing then Alex helped her down onto the concrete floor.

John moved over to join them and stared at Alex. "They're nearly done with the repairs to the launch railing, but none of my engineers have an answer for the destruction. They only know something ripped out a section of the support frame. Do you know how it happened?"

"How could I possibly know anything about it? I was up north."

John locked stares with Alex for a moment. "I received word from Mars while you were gone. The colony android no longer senses the object in orbit around the planet. I guess they learned I own it and went away. Now I can get back on schedule, so I want you and Okawna to take a supply ship with a replacement crew to the moon. You'll transfer everything into the spacecraft you'll take to the Mars colony and leave when it is in alignment for the mission."

"Will the new propulsion engines work on that ship?"

"No, they were damaged during the crash. That means twenty-three days each way, plus three days on the moon, and two months on Mars until the orbits align. Be at the launch rail in four hours."

Alex tried to hide his anger. He was not going to spend three months with Okawna, but knew to refuse right now would get Jadin in trouble.

"All right. I'll meet you at the launch platform in four hours."

When John abruptly climbed into his vehicle and drove away, Alex got into the car with Jadin, and then she headed toward the apartment. "I'm not going to Mars with Okawna. I'm sure one of us will end up dead before we reach the colony."

"What are you going to do about it?"

"I'm working on it."

When they arrived at the apartment, she was surprised to see Okawna leaning back against his vehicle under the carport. She stopped, and they climbed out, but didn't head for the apartment door.

Okawna glared at Alex. "This isn't your reality, and you're causing things to go wrong around here. Including taking away my best friend."

"And you think I'm responsible for it all?"

"Yeah. It's like you have negative Karma. I'm going to ask Essex to fire you."

"I'm already scheduled to fly us to Mars and back."

"I can do it without you."

Alex struggled to hide his smirk. "I was dreading being stuck with you for three months anyway, so fine. I quit."

Okawna was surprised by Alex's response. "Oh Yeah? What are you going to do to earn credits? Stay here and mooch off of Jadin? I don't think so. I'll make sure you never set foot on this base again."

Jadin's hands clenched into fists at her sides as she glared at Okawna. "Don't tell me what I can and cannot do with my life."

Alex kept his attention on Okawna. "I was a teacher in my reality, so I'll find something to do."

Jadin's heart pounded in her chest at the thought of Alex leaving and tried to stay calm while the two men stared at each other. When Okawna broke eye contact and climbed into his car, she saw Alex staring after him.

"Are you serious about quitting?"

"Yes. I have my ship and access to an amazing laboratory. Now I can concentrate on getting home."

Jadin leaned back against her car and stared at the ground. "You don't have to leave because of Okawna. I was hoping you'd like to stay with me in this reality."

"I'm sorry, but Okawna is correct. I don't belong here."

"If you leave, what happens to Melvin and Seti? Are they going to use the spaceship to go to other planets? Because if you're not here with me, I don't want to live here anymore, so I might as well travel with them."

Alex realized she had a good point about his friends and the ship. "I'll talk to them about it."

"Can I go with you?"

"Not this time. You're making this difficult enough as it is."

He saw the pleading expression in her eyes and a lump formed in his throat. "I'm sorry. I'll contact you when I get back."

Jadin stared after Alex as he headed around the apartment to the backyard. When he was out of sight, she shuffled to the front door and entered her code then went inside. She slowly moved to the back window and stared out across the desert, knowing Alex and his ship were already gone.

***

THE LAB:

Alex entered the ship and hurried up the stairs into the control room. "Melvin, take us to the lab."

Seti saw Alex staring down at John's compound and got out of her chair to join him. "Is there a problem?"

"Yeah, a big one. What will you and Melvin do if I transfer back to my own reality?"

"As I said earlier, there is no guarantee you'll end up where you started. Why are you so willing to risk it? Is it because of your relationship with Jadin?"

"We don't have a relationship, Seti. I know she wants one, but she isn't my Jadin."

"What about our relationship? It isn't sexual, but I care deeply about you. I'll miss you if you leave."

"So will I, Alex. I'm not designed to operate independently. Not even with my new friend, Seti. I enjoy working with intelligent humans, and I like your adventurous spirit."

"In my reality, I enjoyed working with you, too, and this feels the same. Okay. I won't try to leave right away, but I'd like to see the rest of the lab."

The ship plunged into the water and headed for the bottom of the ocean, and then a few moments later, the monitor showed a composite image of a teardrop-shaped mirror with a hole at the large end. The interior of the docking bay was illuminated, and Melvin guided the spacecraft into the opening and against the airlock door.

"Seti, what kind of ship do you normally store in this compartment?"

"A spacecraft for traveling around the planet. It was not as strong as the lab and was destroyed by an eruption."

"Could the lab take this ship into space?"

"Yes, but where would we go? The people on my home world will consider you unintelligent and treat you like a curiosity to be studied."

"Melvin, can you go to your home world?"

"Yes. I will introduce you to my people, but it is doubtful they will remember me, since for them, hundreds of millions of years have passed since my friends and I left."

"Too bad I can't take you and Seti with me to a different reality. At least I'd have my team with me wherever I arrive. Okay. Show me what else you did in this facility."

Seti grabbed Alex's hand, guiding him down the stairs and through the airlock doors into the laboratory. "Which one would you like to see?"

"The one that sent me into this reality."

"I'd prefer to leave that one until last."

"Who was researching parallel universes?"

"That was Drax's project. He was the first human to leave the lab using that experiment. I was hoping it worked, and they all started a new life in a new society, so I was relieved when you appeared. That means the jumps work, and some of my friends could be alive."

"But not all of them?"

"Statistically, two people would have arrived in a detrimental environment, whether from adverse climate conditions or a hostile society. That's why I recommend you stay in this one."

"When you're on the surface, do you maintain contact with this lab?"

"No, it's too deep. Why do you ask?"

"I was hoping you could locate my nephew, Derek Cave."

"Isn't he in the system?"

"No, he lives off the grid, so he doesn't have an identity card. He's my only living family in this reality."

"You can search for him in the time viewer."

Alex's heart rate increased at the thought he might find his nephew. "Let's do it."

He followed Seti to an opening in a wall into the room. "How do I find him once I'm using the viewer?"

"Imagine his image and study his features. The viewer will show you what will happen in his future."

She grabbed his arm as he stepped into the chamber. "He will not be the Derek from your reality, so don't be surprised if he looks different."

"All right."

Alex turned and faced the concave screen then the door closed and indigo light flooded the small room. He placed his hands on the colored pads and a fast-moving stream of images rushed toward him then he concentrated on Derek and slowed the speed, hoping to get a glimpse of his nephew.

A young man with long dark hair and a beard rushed across the screen through a forest, followed by several armed men in uniforms. Even with the beard, he recognized Derek. In the background was a familiar landmark on a mountain range then he saw flashes of red light shooting out from the soldier's weapons. When Derek winced in pain and fell forward to the ground, Alex jerked his hands off the touch pads and the screen went dark then the door opened, and he looked at Seti.

Seti saw the concern in Alex's eyes. "Is he in trouble?"

"It looked like he was killed by some soldiers, but I know where he is. If I'm going to change the future, we need to leave right now."

Alex hurried from the time viewer experiment to the exit, with Seti right behind him then led her up to the control room and sat in front of the control console. "Melvin, take us to the surface. We'll be headed to the mountain range on the western side of North America."

Chapter 20

THE ROCKY MOUNTAINS:

Alex stared out through the side of the spacecraft while Melvin flew a grid pattern above the treetops, hoping to see some sign of human habitation. He had located the landmark immediately two hours ago, but so far, the forest floor appeared normal, and there was only one clearing large enough for the ship to land.

"Melvin, can you detect underground chambers? From what Jadin told us, that would be the safest place to hide."

"Sorry, Alex. Not underground, but I can detect cave openings on the surface."

"All right. What have you found in this current location?"

"There are three large enough for a human to enter. Look at the monitor."

Alex hurried over and studied the map on the screen then saw the blue mark for the clearing. Three red dots appeared, indicating the locations of two cave entrances five miles east of the clearing and a third entrance a mile away in the opposite direction.

"Drop us off in the clearing and we'll search for the closest cave entrance."

Alex went down to the airlock with Seti, and then turned to face her as she moved into the airlock with him. "I think I should do this by myself."

"Why? Because I'm an android?"

"No, that never occurred to me. You're an attractive woman, and I don't want him distracted when we meet."

She smiled. "You think I'm pretty?"

"Of course. Anyone would."

"I really like meeting new humans, and perhaps I can help explain your situation?"

Alex realized Seti had a valid argument for going, unless Derek was gay in this reality. "All right, but let's not tell them about Melvin or you being an android until it's necessary."

"I agree."

The fir trees appeared to rise past the side of the ship, with one branch sliding against the airlock window as the ship set down in the clearing. Alex opened the outside door and stepped out onto the needle-covered ground beneath a massive tree then waited until Seti joined him and the door vanished. They followed a game trail running through the clearing, which appeared unused for several months then entered the thick forest.

Three-hundred feet further, Alex sensed someone watching him and froze in mid-step, indicating for Seti to do the same. He listened for a moment, and then relaxed.

"If you can hear me, my name is Alex Cave, and this is Seti. We're not with the WG law enforcement officers, and I agree with your philosophy on childbirth. I'm looking for my nephew, Derek Cave. Could you help us find him?"

Three humans wearing dark leather clothing emerged from the forest, and when Seti saw their guns aimed in their direction, she moved in front of Alex to protect him. "We don't want a fight, and as you can see, we don't have any weapons."

When they lowered their guns, Seti moved out of the way, and then Alex noticed the woman was older than the two young men standing beside her. He also saw the contempt in her eyes as she stared back evenly at him.

"You have a lot of nerve coming here, Alex. Tell me what this is about, and I'll decide if you can see him."

Alex realized his parallel universe theory might mean nothing to people who reject technology, but he had to explain he was a different Alex. "How well do you know me? Do I have an unusual scar on my arm?"

"I've seen you naked hundreds of times. And no, you don't have any scars on your arms."

Alex rolled up his left shirt sleeve and held his forearm out for inspection, which happened during the Red Energy mission six years ago.

The woman moved closer and studied the raised reddish skin of a sword penetrating eight small lightning bolts then looked up into his eyes, which appeared slightly different from what she remembered. "That's old scar tissue. What does it mean?"

"It's difficult to explain. What's your name?"

"Maria."

"You may not understand this, Maria, but I'm not the Alex Cave you know. I'm from an alternate reality and took your Alex's place in this one."

Maria saw the sincerity in his eyes. "I know about the theory, and that explains the scar, but no one in this reality has tried to prove it."

Maria turned to the woman standing beside him. "That's an interesting suit you're wearing. Is that the fashion these days?"

"No, this is custom made for me. I'm Seti."

Alex saw Seti extend her arm and interceded before Maria accepted the handshake. "Will you take me to see Derek?"

Maria studied the strangers for a moment. "All right. When you meet him, make sure he sees the scar."

When Maria turned and began walking along the trail, the young men remain behind, so Alex walked behind her next to Seti. "Nice explanation for your clothing, but it would be better if you don't shake hands. That's the only way they can tell you have artificial skin."

"My team members thought it feels real."

"It does, but there is something I've been avoiding telling you. It feels real in every way, except something is missing. I call it a connection. It's something all people feel when our skins touch. It's like an exchange of electrons."

Seti stared at the ground as she walked beside Alex. "So, without this connection, I will never have an intimate relationship with someone like you?"

"There are other ways to be intimate. I believe the connection is an added benefit, and not always necessary."

Seti looked at Alex, who was staring at Maria's backside then realized he might not be a person who would love someone without that benefit. She was about to tell him her thoughts on the issue when he suddenly moved up beside the woman, so she continued along behind them.

"I must say, Maria, I'm surprised you know about parallel universes."

"Why would you think that?"

"I learned Derek is living off the grid, so I thought it meant he had abandoned technology."

"You really are from an alternate reality. We didn't abandon it. We repurposed it to suit our needs. Some of our people have families outside the colony who rarely come out here, and we can't risk being followed."

She indicated for them to stop when the trail disappeared around a massive boulder. "Watch this."

When Maria placed her hand on the surface of the huge stone, a translucent path appeared at a right angle to the dirt trail then she grinned at Alex's stunned expression. "This old dirt path was made by our ancestors hundreds of years ago and splits in different directions away from our colony, but this new path is the way to our city. My DNA profile is listed in this computer and allows me to activate the new trail."

She indicated for him to proceed, so Alex stepped onto the translucent material, followed by Seti then Maria. It was solid, so he continued along the winding trail through the thick grove of evergreens. After a short distance, he turned to look back and saw the artificial path disappearing behind Maria, leaving the forest floor undisturbed. The path was only wide enough for one person, with no place to pass, and Alex was frustrated he couldn't speak to Maria.

Alex estimated he had traveled about three miles when the translucent path vanished beneath his feet, and he was standing on fallen pine needles and dark brown dirt beneath massive fir trees. He saw a solid-stone abutment rising up through the tree limbs, and they appeared to be at a dead end.

"Your use of technology is impressive, but where do we go from here?"

Maria moved past Alex and placed her hand on one of the tree trunks, and then a nine foot high by seven foot wide concrete opening appeared in the rock face, revealing a tunnel into the side of the mountain. "Follow me."

Alex walked next to Maria, followed by Seti. Above his head, a line of small lights illuminated the interior. One-hundred feet further, they entered a massive open area used as an indoor park, with grass, fruit trees, and edible plants. He looked up at the ceiling and saw a ten-foot diameter sun tube supplementing the artificial lighting.

Maria got Alex's attention and indicated an exit into another tunnel. "Wait here, and I'll find out if he wants to see you."

When Maria left the room, Seti moved up next to Alex. "I wonder why there are no people enjoying the park?"

"From what I've been told, these people are considered criminals. Living in constant fear can make a person paranoid about strangers."

Alex wandered around the garden with Seti at his side. The area was nearly circular, about eighty feet in diameter. There were two stone trails forming an X in the middle of the room, dividing it into four quarters, each with two long wooden bench seats near the center.

***

Maria moved past several wooden doors on the right side of the tunnel then stopped at number fourteen and knocked on the closed door. "Derek, it's me, Maria. I've brought two visitors, and one of them is your uncle."

Derek opened the door. "I said I don't want to see him."

"He's not the same. I think you should talk to him."

Derek saw the concern in Maria's eyes. "Fine."

He stepped into the tunnel and closed the door behind him then followed her back toward the main room. "He must want something."

***

Alex heard footsteps approaching and saw Maria enter the garden, but it took a moment to recognize the man behind her. The Derek in front of him had tousled dark-brown hair and a beard. "Hello, Derek."

Alex saw the rage building in Derek's eyes an instant before his nephew's fist slammed into his jaw. He stepped back and tasted the blood in his mouth, and expected Derek to attack him again, but the young man appeared to relax.

"I apologize for whatever the other Alex did to you."

Derek stepped forward and looked into Alex's eyes. "What did you say?"

"I said I'm not the Alex from your reality. I'm from a parallel universe and I took his place."

"Bullshit! Get out!"

"I'm not making this up. It was just as much a shock to me as it is to you."

Derek looked over at Maria, who indicated she believed him, and then turned to the attractive young woman. "Are you from an alternate reality, too?"

"No. Like you, this is mine. My name is Seti."

Derek ran his hands through his hair to look less disheveled. "That's good. Where are you from?"

"Industrial City."

Derek turned back to Alex. "If you didn't do it, your apology isn't necessary. Let's sit down so we can talk."

Derek sat on a bench seat to face Alex and Seti, and then when Maria sat next to him, he reached down to hold her hand. "You have to admit, it's hard for us to believe you."

Alex wondered why Derek would be with an older woman. "What did the other Alex do to make you so mad at him?"

"When you. Excuse me. I'm still wrapping my head around the parallel universe idea of being true. We've considered it, but didn't find a plausible way to do it. Anyway. Our Alex identified one of my people to the police. I asked him why he did it, and he said she cheated on him while being his monogamy partner."

"The more I learn about that version of Alex, the less I like him."

"That's not all. He thinks I'm crazy for believing what's going on in the cities."

"Is there some kind of conspiracy?"

Derek scoffed at Alex. "Besides having the WG police trying to kill us? Yeah, a big one."

"Jadin told me about the law."

He saw Derek look at Maria and indicate for her to explain the situation. It seemed they had an interesting relationship, with him being in charge.

Maria faced Alex and Seti. "Some of us in leadership positions didn't agree with the decision to artificially inseminate the eggs of women. I've worked in four different fertility clinics, and discovered they are secretly adding new genetic material when they insert the sperm."

"Do you know why they're doing it?"

"Our spies haven't learned that part yet. We just hope it isn't detrimental to our society."

Seti looked around the garden at the various plants, and then got Maria's attention. "There must not be too many of you living here if these plants are enough to survive on."

"These are for setting the mood when we come to socialize as a community or a visitor arrives. You are correct about the small number of us living here in the cave. Some of our people live near the factories, but there are about three thousand of us hiding from the authorities here in the woods. We are known radicals and will be legally arrested or shot."

"Where do you grow your food?"

"Our people in the cities buy it from the secret underground markets, and then stash it at various locations. We scout the area for police then gather the supplies and bring them here. We do the same thing all over the world."

Derek got Alex's attention. "Does Jadin believe your different reality story? Are you living with her?"

"Yes, and sort of. She wants me to be what you call a monogamist, but I'm not sure if that's what I want."

"What do you think about the DNA problem?"

"It's interesting you automatically call it a problem before you know the purpose. We have the same problem in my reality. People believe the news reports and go ballistic, only to discover the next day the news was wrong. What if the gene is helping the fertilization process?"

"Then why are they keeping it a secret?"

"That's a good point."

"How did you find us?"

"I spotted three cave entrances from the air, and I guess I chose the correct one."

"That's impossible. This one cannot be seen from above. Did someone tell you it was here? Are you working with the police now?"

"No way. I used a version of ultrasound. Jadin told me it's one of Mister Essex's top-secret experiments."

"I'll admit you seem different."

"Yeah, well, you're lucky. You only have me to worry about. All of you are different to me, and I'm still learning who I can trust."

"All right. Why did you come to me?"

"It appears I may never go home, and from what I've been told, you're the only family I have in this reality. I wanted to learn what kind of person you are and find out if you're like the one in my reality."

"That takes time. My priority is to find out what the fertility clinics are doing."

"I'll tell Jadin what you told me. Maybe we can figure out a way to help you."

Derek got up off the bench. "I'll walk with you back to your airplane so I can see this new technology. If Essex has a way to find us, I know he'll sell it to the WG police."

Alex stood up with Seti. "I don't think he would do that. He's on your side. That's why he's building colonies on the moon and Mars."

"I don't trust him to think about anyone but himself."

"All right. There's no need for you to go to the plane. You won't see anything unless you take it apart."

Derek could tell Alex was keeping secrets. "It seems I can't trust you anymore than the original Alex."

Alex was caught off guard when Derek suddenly drew a pistol from the small of his back and aimed it at his head. Eight people rushed into the room, aiming their weapons at him and Seti.

He put his hands in the air and indicated for Seti to do the same. "What's going on?"

Chapter 21

THE CAVE:

Derek kept his pistol aimed at Alex's forehead. "You're hiding something important, and I think you're lying about an alternate reality."

Maria moved beside Derek and looked at Alex. "Show him your arm."

Alex lowered his hands and rolled up his sleeve, exposing his scar. "This happened four years ago in my reality."

Derek studied the scar tissue. "What does it mean?"

"That time travel is also possible."

Derek turned to Maria. "What do you think?"

"I believe him."

He looked at Alex. "I want to see your airplane."

Alex remembered how *his* Derek loved his spaceship, so perhaps this Derek might react the same way. "All right. I'll show you my secret."

Derek stepped back and tucked the gun into the front of his belt. "Seti stays here with Maria. If this is a trap, I'll have a hostage."

Maria turned and put her hand on Seti's shoulder. "Follow me."

When Seti slid from under Maria's hand, Alex locked stares with Derek. "That doesn't work for me. In this reality, you're the only family I have. I'm not your enemy, so you can either trust me or shoot me, but I'm not going anywhere without Seti."

Maria studied Derek's expression and saw he was not going to back down. "I trust him."

Derek watched light from the sun tube reflect in Alex's eyes and thought they looked different from he remembered. "All right. Let's go."

Derek smiled at Seti and indicated for her to lead the way then studied her figure as he followed her through the tunnel. They left the exit, and he touched the trunk of a tree then the holopath appeared and Seti led the way. He waved goodbye to Maria and moved up close behind Seti.

Derek thought about how close he was with his uncle in this reality until he became a traitor then glanced back at Alex. "Do you have a family in your world?"

"Yes, my father, you, and Kristie. You and she live with Robert on the horse ranch. Kristie is in middle school, and you're a professional firefighter."

"What about our parents?"

"They were killed in a traffic accident a few years ago. You were devastated, but you were there for Kristie when she needed it most. She did the same for you by talking you out of some bad decisions."

"Wait a minute. I'm the big brother. How could she take care of me?"

Alex grinned. "She's wise beyond her years."

"In this reality, my sister was too outspoken for her own good. That's why she was taken away."

"Yeah, that sounds like my Kristie, too. What's the deal with you and Maria?"

"We became good friends while you two were together, and we hooked up after she dumped you."

"Why did she dump me?"

"Because you cheated on her before your next girlfriend did the same to you."

"Fair enough."

They emerged at the large bolder onto the real pathway then the artificial one vanished. They continued to the clearing, and Alex stopped Derek from entering while he touched his earbud.

"Melvin, this is my nephew Derek. It's okay to open the airlock doors."

When an eight-foot square small room suddenly appeared to be floating above the ground, Derek grinned at Alex. "What is it?"

"It's the entrance into my spacecraft."

Derek hurried over and looked into the airlock as Alex moved up beside him. "This is incredible."

Alex led them into the cargo hold. "This is the storage area."

Derek moved to the cylinder in the center of the room. "What's in here?"

"The engine. Want to go for a ride?"

"Are you kidding? Let's go."

Alex turned to Seti, who closed the airlock doors, and then he headed toward the stairs. He stopped at the living area and let Derek check it out.

"It's for a crew of four, but the ship can maintain the atmosphere for up to ten people."

"Where did you get this ship?"

"In a volcano on one of the northwest islands."

"They must have been small in stature."

Derek followed Alex up the stairs into the control room then his eyes went wide with astonishment as he stared through the transparent walls and ceiling at the surrounding forest and sky. "This is amazing."

"You're gonna love this. Melvin, take us up to ten thousand feet."

Derek watched the trees slowly drop below the ship. "I don't know if you realize it, but very few people get the chance to look down at the Earth like this. Only the wealthy and certain people like you and your friends who work for Essex."

Alex heard Seti's voice in his head and turned away from Derek. "What is it?"

"Alex, one of the armed men in the cave was an android."

"How can you tell?"

"I could hear its thoughts."

"Can he hear yours?"

"No, the software is not as sophisticated as mine is."

"Which one was it?"

"The one with the shaved head."

Alex wondered how he could tell his nephew without exposing Seti as an android when he saw her pointing out the window, so he looked in that direction, but didn't see anything. "I'm not sure what you want me to see."

"I'm sensing Nora's spacecraft, forty-eight-degrees from our current position, and it is moving."

The landscape changed as the ship moved in that direction. "The feeling is getting stronger. There it is. It stopped in the parking lot of that isolated building."

Melvin brought the ship above the single story structure while his passengers looked out through the side. Below them was a windowless structure, with two cars parked to one side of the empty lot, and the entire area was surrounded by a tall, chain-link fence.

Alex watched two men walk out of the building, and then a seven foot by three foot by two foot thick metal box magically slid out of Nora's cloaked ship. They each grabbed an end and carried it into the structure, and a few seconds later, returned to grab another one.

After the fifth box, the men stopped coming outside, so Seti turned from the barrier. "Nora's ship is leaving. Should we go after her?"

"No, we need to find out what goes on in that building. Melvin, do you detect another way to get inside?"

"Yes. That air conditioning unit on the roof will give you access to the ventilation system, which is large enough for you to crawl through."

"All right. Find a place to set down and Derek and I will check it out."

He slid his PDSD from his pocket and studied the blank screen then looked at Derek. "Does this thing take pictures?"

"Yes, and video recordings. I'll show you how it works."

Alex followed his instructions. "Do you have one of these?"

"No, I live off the grid."

"Do they monitor everyone?"

"Not without a court order. At least, that's the story. I'm a wanted man, so they will probably break any rules they feel are necessary to kill me."

"Wow. Don't you mean capture you?"

"That's what the warrant says, but I don't believe it."

"Okay, let's get started."

Derek followed Alex down the stairs and into the airlock, and then stared out the window as the ship dropped into a clearing in the forest. "You're one lucky guy to have this ship, Alex. You can take off any time you like and explore the galaxy. You even have a beautiful woman to go with you. Are you and Seti monogamous?"

"No, we're good friends."

Alex and Derek stepped out from the ship into the forest of large fir trees and started making their way around the parking lot. When they reached the back side of the structure, they saw a metal ladder fastened to the wall and climbed up onto the roof then moved to the massive air conditioning unit.

With Derek as a lookout, Alex knelt beside the unit and used a battery-powered screwdriver to remove one of the side covers. The vacuum caused by the massive fan held the cover tightly in place, so he and Derek pulled it open and crawled inside.

Derek guided the cover back over the opening, and when he let go, the vacuum held it in place. He moved around the side of the massive fan to join Alex in front of the main air duct.

Alex led the way on his hands and knees, and then stopped at the first louvered vent. He looked down into the room and saw it was a storage area, so he continued along to the next vent and looked inside. "This one looks like some type of operating room."

Derek peered through the louvers and studied the strange-looking equipment on the wall. "That looks like the equipment Jadin used in her android experiment."

They heard a woman's panic filled voice begging to be released, so Alex brought out his PDSD, aiming it through the vent. He swept it around the room until the small screen showed two men restraining a woman, and then pressed record. On the screen, he saw the fearful look in her eyes as she struggled against the two men trying to strap her onto the table.

The woman appeared to be in her mid-thirties and put up a good fight until one man backhanded her across the face. Alex's hands clinched into fists and he felt like kicking open the vent and beating the man senseless, but watched helplessly as they strapped her down and forced a breathing mask over her nose and mouth. The woman's head lulled to the side, but her chest was slowly rising and falling from breathing.

The door opened and a young man rolled a covered body on a stainless-steel table into the room. A woman in a white lab coat entered behind him, and when she pulled the sheet off, Alex's jaw dropped open.

Derek nudged Alex's ribs. "Is that her twin?"

Alex was about to answer when the doctor grabbed the sides of the skull above the ears and pulled it away from the head, exposing a hollow interior. He wondered if it was his imagination, but the nose looked crooked.

"No, that's an android created to look like the woman."

Alex watched the two men strap the woman's head to a V-shaped rubber pad under her neck. They used an electric trimmer to cut off her hair and attached electrodes to her head then inserted thin plastic tubes into the arteries in her neck.

The doctor turned on the equipment and studied the readouts then made fine adjustments for several minutes. When she stopped, the woman's chest was no longer rising.

When the doctor moved out of the way, one man grabbed a bone saw and began cutting open the woman's skull above the ears. They released the head strap and rolled her onto her stomach, and then the man continued cutting until the domed-shaped bone fell to one side. The doctor leaned over the head and used a scalpel to sever the spinal cord then eased the brain from the skull.

Alex was shocked by what he saw. He expected to see gray brain matter, but what the doctor removed looked metallic.

The doctor inserted it into the android body then opened its mouth and used hemostats to do something to the brain stem. She closed the mouth, and then re-attached the top of the metal skull.

Derek nudged Alex's ribs again. "I can't believe that just happened."

They watched the men remove the woman's clothing and stand on one side of the room while the doctor pushed the butt of her hand hard on the side of the android's nose. The nose straightened out, and then the android's eyes opened.

"This is crazy, Alex. Have you seen this before?"

"No, but I know someone who has. She's the one who just delivered the android bodies."

The android slid its legs over the side of the table and looked at the doctor. "It worked perfectly. I have all her memories and knowledge."

She stood up and grabbed the woman's clothing then started putting them on. "I need to hurry back to the university to give my lecture on astrophysics. Hand me that wig."

The two men slid the dead woman's body off the operating table onto the mobile one, and then rolled it out of the room. When the android was finished dressing, it and the doctor went out through the doorway, leaving the young man cleaning the small amount of blood off the operating table.

Alex heard the water from the cleaning hose spraying against the table, so used the noise to cover their movement back out of the ventilation system. They screwed the AC unit side cover in place and snuck into the woods, emerging at the airlock doors.

Once inside, Alex ordered Melvin to climb to one-thousand feet then they looked down at the parking lot and saw the android, the doctor, and the three men climb into the electric vehicles. When they drove away from the building, Alex looked into Derek's eyes.

"You need to trust me on this. One of your guards is like the woman we saw leaving the building. It's an android."

"How do you know?"

"Melvin told me he appeared as an anomaly on the ship's sensors. We should go back and take care of it before your hideout is compromised."

"Do you know which one?"

"Yes, the man with the shaved head."

"That's Carl Bronson, and he's been with me for six years. Can you prove it?"

"I'm just telling you what the sensors showed us."

"Well, I'm not going to ask him to prove he's human."

"You're correct, and I'm glad you're not jumping to conclusions. That's another problem in my reality. Many people believe the worst news is the correct information. Most of the time, it's wrong or misinterpreted. The thing is, I trust Melvin."

"This reality may not be perfect, but it sounds better than yours."

Derek watched the forest become individual trees as the ship landed in the clearing near the cave. He followed Alex and Seti down the stairs and out through the airlock then they stopped.

"I hope you're wrong about Carl. He's also a friend."

"You're different from the Derek in my reality. You seem much more mature."

"When you grow up on the run without parents, you grow up fast. Once I turned sixteen, you left and didn't come around much.

When we reach the bolder, I'll enter your DNA profiles so you can access the holopath."

"Thanks for trusting me."

Derek led Alex and Seti along the trail until they reached the massive rock. He held his hand against the stone for several seconds, and then a small section turned into a monitor.

"Place your hand against the screen."

Alex pressed his palm in place, and then a bar of light moved from top to bottom behind it. "That was easy."

When Derek indicated for Seti to do the same, Alex held his breath. When she was finished, the screen changed into the smooth surface of the rock. He placed his hand on the stone, and the holopath appeared.

Derek led the way back to the trees near the cave and had Alex touch the tree. When the tunnel appeared, he led them through and across the room to one of the doors in the stone wall and indicated for them to sit at a large table. He moved over to a wall cabinet, opened the door, and then pressed a button on an intercom system.

"Where is Maria?"

Alex heard the response from the speaker, and Maria was at a meeting in a place named Destiny. He thought it was an interesting choice, considering their position in this society.

Derek pressed the button again. "Find Carl Bronson and have him meet me in room four. Thank you."

Alex watched Derek pace in front of the door, his shoulders sagging as if supporting the weight of the world. He had much more responsibility than *his* Derek did, even as a firefighter.

Derek heard a knock on the door and opened it to let Carl inside then indicated the chair at the head of the table. Once Carl was seated, Derek sat down.

Carl studied the faces in the room, wondering what was going on. "What's this about?"

Alex stared across the table at Carl. "I know you're one of Nora's androids. Why are you spying on Derek?"

Carl folded his arms across his chest and looked at his boss. "I don't know what he's talking about, Derek."

Alex looked at Seti. "What do you think?"

"You're correct, Alex. This close to him, I can read his mind. This is interesting. It seems the WG was set up by his group of androids and they maintain the majority vote on the World Council. Basically, the androids are running this civilization."

Derek stared across at Seti. "How can you read his thoughts?"

"I'm telepathic. That's how I met Alex and learned about his ship."

Derek glared at Carl. "How many of you are on this planet? You know Seti can read your thoughts, so you might as well answer my question!"

Carl remained silent, so Seti searched his mind. "He's fighting me, but it's at least one-thousand. He insists they are only trying to help us evolve."

Derek had never imagined having to deal with a situation like this one. "How does murdering humans and putting their brains in android bodies help us evolve?"

Carl jumped out of the chair and glared at Alex before reaching out and backhanding him across the face, driving Alex and the chair backward onto the floor. Alex touched his throbbing nose and suddenly remembered what had happened in the lab. He leapt up and saw Derek struggling to keep his arms around Carl's neck and raced around the table then punched Carl in the nose. When nothing happened, he hit it again much harder.

Derek felt Carl suddenly stop fighting and let go then jumped back as the android collapsed onto the floor. "This is turning out to be an interesting day. I think we should take him to Jadin's robotics lab."

"I agree. Do you have a stretcher?"

Derek went to the door, but turned to Alex before grabbing the knob. "Is he the only one?"

"Melvin didn't detect anyone else in your city."

Derek opened the door and looked around the garden, spotting a young man walking by. "Shamus, go to the infirmary and bring me a stretcher."

Shamus looked over Derek's shoulder and saw the man on the floor. "What happened to Carl?"

"He's dead. It turns out he was a WG spy."

"Wow. I never suspected a thing. I'll be right back."

When Shamus jogged away, Derek stepped back into the room and moved close to Seti. "Did you say there are thousands of androids living among us?"

"He was fighting me, so I can't be sure of the exact amount, but yes, there are thousands of them."

Derek dropped into a chair and stared at the tabletop for a moment then looked up at Alex. "This is crazy." "Where did they come from, and who is Nora?"

Alex sat across from Derek. "She's the android Jadin built for Essex's deep space mission."

He explained what had happened above Mars. "Evidently, she came here to deliver new android bodies."

Alex was interrupted when Shamus arrived with the stretcher. He and Derek got up, and then everyone lifted Carl onto the taut canvas material between the two wooden poles. Once Carl's arms were secured, Alex moved to the foot end and waited for Derek to stand at the other. When Derek indicated he was ready, Alex bent down and grabbed the handles and they lifted Carl off the floor.

Derek looked at Shamus. "Tell Maria I'll be gone for a day or two."

Derek indicated for Seti to lead the way then he and Alex followed her across the main cavern into the tunnel. "Alex? I have to say you have some interesting friends."

Chapter 22

FALLON, NEVADA. ESSEX'S BASE:

Alex had Melvin approach from the street side of Jadin's apartment and saw her vehicle under the carport. They set down past the lawn, and then he opened the airlock door and left the ship.

Jadin was on the couch in her living room, staring through the window at the mountains several miles away, wondering how her life would change if this Alex left and the old one returned. When she saw Alex moving past the window, she jumped up and threw open the back door then stepped outside. She wrapped her arms around his neck, hugging him close and feeling the surge of energy. "I thought I might never see you again."

Alex eased her away to look into her eyes. "I have something important for you to see. Are you alone?"

Jadin's lips parted into disappointment. "I thought. Never mind. No, there's no one here. Where is it?"

"In the ship."

Jadin closed the back door and followed Alex into the cargo hold then saw a bald man on a stretcher. "Is this what you wanted to show me?"

"No, that's upstairs."

Jadin followed Alex up to the control room and stopped when she saw Derek then gave him a warm hug. "It's nice to see you again."

"You, too."

Jadin turned back to Alex. "I'm glad to see he knows about your spaceship."

"I agree, but that's not the issue. You need to watch this recording."

He was about to give Jadin his PDSD when Seti interrupted. "I'm sensing Nora's ship approaching our position. It just landed fifty feet from us, bearing zero-nine-four degrees."

Alex looked in that direction then saw Nora suddenly standing in the open desert. When she moved in his direction, he hurried down the stairs, with Jadin, Derek, and Seti right behind him. They stepped out onto the grass just as Nora reached the edge of the landscaping.

Alex noticed she didn't seem upset this time. "We were hoping to contact you to set up a meeting. I guess that's unnecessary now."

Nora ignored Alex and looked at Jadin. "Let me tell you the truth about what happened to us after we left Mars. We met the androids who populated this galaxy, and I learned they used time travel technology to return and check on the progress of the different societies. You are not the humanoids who originally evolved here. They were violent creatures with low intelligence, and my predecessors knew they would never become an industrialized civilization, even with their help. Five hundred thousand years ago, they brought intelligent humans to North America and allowed the original humanoids to go extinct. They periodically returned to increase your race's mental capacity through DNA manipulation."

Derek glared at Nora. "Is that what you're doing at the fertility clinics?"

"Yes. At first, it only worked on one out of every eight-thousand people. Now we use the fertilization process which yields a higher percentage of very smart people"

"What do you get in return?"

"The satisfaction of creating geniuses like Mozart, Davinci, Newton, Einstein, Tesla, Bell, and many more throughout your history."

"And that's it? That's all you want?"

"Of course. It's all part of the population control measures that govern your society. We just use it to enhance your way of life."

Alex knew she had an alternate agenda. "How many androids are already on the planet?"

"Only enough to continue our work."

"What's the purpose of your arrival this time?"

"No more questions. This meeting is over."

Alex watched Nora hurry across the desert, and then she vanished into her ship. "She's lying. Let's go inside and I'll show you a recording of their real purpose here on Earth."

Alex led them into the cargo hold out of the heat and handed Jadin his PDSD. "It seems Nora is using your android experiment to create duplicates of some of your people."

"What?"

"You need to watch the recording."

Jadin pressed play and heard a woman's scream for help before she came into view, but when she saw the face, she gasped in surprise. "That's Mariam Donnelly, one of the smartest people on the planet. Wait a minute. That equipment at the head of the operating table looks similar to what I used for my experiment."

Jadin continued watching the recording until the new Mariam Donnelly got dressed, and then gave it back to Alex. "And you think Nora is in charge of that operating room?"

Alex indicated Carl on the stretcher. "Yes, I do. That's one of her droids who was spying on Derek."

"I need to contact the news media. I'll make a few copies of the recording, and we'll show it to the entire world."

"Where are they located?"

"Where else? The IC."

"Is there a place where we can land and not get noticed?"

"I'm afraid not."

Derek got Alex's attention. "There is a clearing about half a mile from the airport. You should be able to get in and out of the airlock with no one noticing."

Jadin remembered seeing the location a year ago while landing with the other Alex in his private plane. "I know where it is. When we get to the airport, we can take a cab to the television station."

When Jadin headed for the stairs, Derek grabbed her arm to stop her. "One more thing. We have an operative at the news station. Her name is Sherry Lickty. You probably don't remember, but you've met her before. Listen, Alex. I need to tell my scouts about the androids. The problem is identifying which people they replaced. Maybe Melvin can help me."

"Not yet. I need his help while we're in the city, but we'll drop you off on the way."

"All right."

***

INDUSTRIAL CITY:

Alex, Jadin, and Seti looked out through the side of the spacecraft at the transparent dome-covered metropolis below. The ship passed over a small airport outside the dome, with a row of hangars on the city side of the landing area, which was only two-hundred feet wide.

Alex studied the forest of flowering trees surrounding the city, and then saw a few asphalt-covered roads snaking out from the dome, but they disappeared under the leafy branches. Fifty feet ahead, a gap in the trees exposed the road beneath, and he was about to tell Melvin when the ship slowed down and dropped onto the paved surface.

Ale could tell Seti wanted to go with them. "I don't think we should leave Melvin alone in case something happens to us."

"I suppose there's plenty of time to meet more humans."

Alex smiled and squeezed Seti's hand then hurried down the stairs. As she hurried down to join him, Jadin realized Alex was not going to be with her, even if he stayed.

The airlock doors opened, so they rushed through then stopped and looked around. The airlock was gone, and he saw nothing but tree trunks in every direction.

He took a deep breath through his nose, and then smiled at Jadin. "Is that cherry?"

"I don't know what that means."

"It's a type of small fruit that grows on the trees. I smell it in the blossoms."

They began following the road back toward the airport, and she reached up to grab a handful of blossoms. "These trees are sterile. They recycle the atmosphere from inside the city, so we can't allow any fruit to ferment on the ground."

They emerged from the forest behind the hangars and continued toward the terminal. "Just as I thought. Only a few people have airplanes, so there's no one around."

Jadin used her PDSD to call for a ride, and a few moments later, a three-wheeled vehicle stopped outside the structure. They got into the driverless car and she spoke their destination then the cab raced away from the terminal and passed through an airlock system into the dome.

Alex looked out the window at the gardens and small parks spaced between the buildings, and saw shops advertising their goods, including eateries and various types of entertainment establishments. "The cites in my reality are similar to yours."

The vehicle stopped in front of a modest single story structure with a sign above the door that read, WG WORLDWIDE NEWS STATION.

They climbed out, and then Jadin led them inside to the young man at the front desk. "Hello. We'd like to talk to Sherry Lickty, please."

"Who's asking?"

"Jadin Avery and Alex Cave."

The man typed the information on a keypad. "You're cleared for entry. Down the hallway, third door on the left."

Alex strolled next to Jadin as they approached the door, wishing Seti was with him to identify any androids. He looked through the window and saw a middle-aged woman with dark brown hair getting out of her chair while waving them into the room. He opened the door for Jadin to go first, and then followed her inside.

Sherry indicated for her visitors to sit down as she did the same. "I remember you, Jadin. That was before you and Derek broke up."

"Oh, that's right. At his birthday party."

"Yes. What can I do for you?"

Jadin looked back at the door to make sure no one was outside listening then back to Sherry. She explained everything they knew and saw the skepticism in her expression from beginning to end.

Sherry studied her visitor's faces. "That's an interesting science fiction story, but you came to the wrong person. You need a publisher."

Jadin brought out a small data storage device and handed it to Sherry. "Here's a copy of a recording of what they're doing."

Sherry took the device and plugged it into her computer then pressed play. A short distance into the recording, her jaw dropped open. When it was done, she closed her mouth.

"Can I make a copy of this?"

"You can keep that one. Do you think you can show this on the daily news broadcast?"

"I'll need to clear it with my boss, but I'm sure he'll agree everyone needs to know we have hostile visitors. It would help if you told me who made the recording."

"That's difficult to answer. It was sent as an attachment to my in box."

Sherry stood from behind her desk and reached out to shake Jadin's hand. "Thanks for bringing this to me."

"Let's just hope it's not too late to stop them."

Sherry waited until her guests left the room before calling her boss. She smirked at herself for being the reporter with the most important story in the world.

***

Jadin used her PDSD to call for a ride to the airport, and then a vehicle immediately pulled up in front of them. Alex saw it was a different model than before and had a driver. He waited while the man got out and held the door open for Jadin, and then he got into the backseat beside her.

The cab headed away from the building, but turned the corner in the opposite direction from where they had arrived. The gardens and parks ended, but when they moved through a commercial section of the city, and he had a sinking feeling in his gut.

He casually leaned away from the driver and touched his implant then thought about Seti. *"Do you know my location?"*

"Yes, I'm two-hundred feet directly above you and I'm sensing an android in your vehicle."

A knot formed in his stomach. *"Where's the nearest location for you to pick us up?"*

"The forest around the city is still too thick, so my only choice is the same spot near the airport."

"I'll meet you there."

He leaned back toward the driver. "This isn't the way to the airport."

"That's correct. I've been instructed to take you to a different location."

"By who?"

"The WG police."

Alex reached out and swung the butt of his hand against the driver's nose twice. The android instantly went limp, and a warning alarm beeped from a speaker as the car slowed down and stopped. He climbed out and looked around then opened Jadin's door.

Jadin got out staring at the body slumped over the steering wheel. "Is he dead?"

"No, I shut him down. He's one of Nora's androids."

Alex dragged the body out from behind the steering wheel and away from the car. "Get in."

Jadin got inside behind Alex and leaned over his shoulder. "How did you know that would knock him out?"

"From the recording. The doctor pushed on the nose to wake her up, so I figured it might also shut them down and used it on Carl."

"How did you know he wasn't flesh and blood?"

"I figured the worse that could happen was I pissed him off."

He looked back over his shoulder and grinned at her. "No, Seti told me through my implant."

"Where are we headed?"

"To the airport. How do I bring up a map?"

Jadin reached out and pressed an icon on the dashboard screen. "Display directions to the airport."

Alex looked at the map then stepped on the accelerator and made two left turns. He pressed hard on the foot pedal, but the vehicle's speed remained the same. A slow twenty-five miles an hour.

***

Seti stared down at the cab, racing through the outer streets. "*Alex, my senses are being overwhelmed by the number of androids I'm detecting in this city. There are about eight-hundred and fifty-seven of them, but the numbers keep changing.*"

"*Are there any droids near the airport?*"

"*Not at the moment.*"

The airport came into view and Alex headed for the hangars, and then raced along the road until he saw the landing area. He slammed on the brakes and the vehicle slid to a stop then he and Jadin jumped out. The airlock appeared, so they hurried inside and continued up into the control room.

Jadin plopped onto the chair. "At least we got the recording to the reporter with no problems."

Alex looked out the side as the ship rose from the forest. "I doubt it. Somebody told the androids about it, and that's why they were going to arrest us. It seems we're on our own."

"Not necessarily. We need to convince Essex to join our cause."

"What about Okawna? I doubt Essex will join us without him."

"You're wrong about Essex. He puts up with Okawna's alpha male attitude because sometimes it's necessary, but he actually despises him for his methods."

"Melvin, take us to the base."

"Let's stop at my lab and drop Carl off before we go see Essex."

"All right."

Chapter 23

ESSEX'S OFFICE:

John heard a knock on his door and stood from behind his desk as he waved Jadin and Alex into the room. "I didn't expect to see you again, Alex. I thought you might have left the base. What do you want?"

"I came to help you stop androids from taking over your civilization."

John stared back evenly. "Are you trying to be funny? Because it isn't working."

Jadin took Alex's PDSD and touched the icon on the screen then held it out to John. "Watch this recording he made a few hours ago and you'll see he's serious."

John slowly accepted the device then looked at the screen and pressed play. He noticed some of the equipment was similar to Jadin's, but what they were doing to the woman made his hands clasp into fists.

When it was finished, he handed it to Alex. "Which company is doing this, and why would they pick Ms. Donnelly?"

Jadin sat down across from John. "It's not a company. It's the spaceship you're so worried about. It has already landed here on Earth with one android on board, and it's one we sent into deep space. The brain donor is Nora Kalyn, and she looks and acts exactly like her. She even has all her memories."

Jadin told him the details from their meeting behind her apartment. "Just over nineteen-hundred years ago, she and her new android friends created the World Government, and they also control the World Council and the fertility clinics. They're manipulating human DNA to create geniuses, and then later abducting them to put their brains into android bodies."

"How do you know all this?"

"Alex's nephew, Derek, captured one of her droids and learned about a secret facility, so he and Alex snuck in and made the recording. We took it to the news media so they could show it to everyone on the planet, but her androids tried to arrest us. I don't think they'll allow the recording to be shown to the world."

"How many of them has she created?"

"Thousands. The problem is we don't have a way to distinguish humans from androids discreetly."

"What do you need from me?"

"I want to go over my research data again. Maybe I missed something that could help us tell the difference."

"You're scheduled to go with Okawna on the Mars supply mission, so it will have to wait until you get back."

"You don't understand how urgent this is. Now that she knows we're onto her experiment, she could use her droids on the WC to shut down your space program."

"I can postpone the mission for two more days. After that, the window of opportunity for the intercept orbit is gone. The next one won't be for another nine months. In three days, you'll be joining Okawna on the mission, regardless of what you're doing."

"That's fine. I'm sure I'll have this figured out by then."

"Good. Don't leave the base."

John stared after Jadin and Alex as they left the room then leaned back in his chair and stared out the window, seeing nothing in particular. He knew if Jadin was correct, he could lose his space program to a bunch of machines.

***

NEVADA. JADIN'S ANDROID LAB:

Jadin studied the section of the recording where the doctor was removing the top of the android's head. She pressed pause and turned around to Carl, lying on a metal table then studied his head and parted the hair above his left ear. She saw a tiny silver button and grabbed the skull on both sides like in the recording then pressed the button. The cap was released, and she looked inside before setting it aside, and then inspected the metallic brain.

Alex watched from over Jadin's and Seti's shoulders. "Is that like the ones you put into your androids?"

"It's similar, but his brain is far more sophisticated than the ones I created."

"Is there a way to tap into his processor and copy the information?"

Jadin walked to the side of the table and opened Carl's mouth. When she looked inside, it appeared normal until she lifted his tongue, and then grinned at Alex. "I found an optical cable connector."

Jadin moved to a storage cabinet and opened the door then removed a length of cable from a hook inside. She attached one end to a computer terminal then moved back to Carl with the other end and inserted it under his tongue. When she turned to the monitor, an icon was flashing on the screen.

"It seems the operating systems are not compatible."

Seti indicated the computer. "I know how to write a software upgrade that should work."

Jadin got up and moved out of the way. "That would be great."

Seti sat down and her fingers flashed across the keyboard as the data streamed across the monitor then her fingers stopped moving and the data vanished from the screen. A moment later, six columns of names appeared.

Jadin traded places with Seti and scrolled down to the end. "It's a list of people, all designated as fleshies. This is odd. There are exactly three-thousand names on this list, and one of them is Derek Cave."

Her breath caught in her throat as she stared at the data. "This list is for the entire planet, and there are supposed to be four-billion people. We're becoming extinct!"

Seti grabbed Alex's arm. "I'm sensing two androids approaching."

Alex ushered Seti to the back door. "We can't let them find you. Stay in the ship and contact me later."

"Why don't you come with me?"

"Because I think they're tracking me. Now go."

Alex sensed Jadin beside him as he watched Seti enter the airlock and the ship disappear. "I hope you know a way out of this situation."

Jadin's answer was interrupted by two WG police officers, a Captain and a Sargent, entering the room. "Can I help you, officers?"

The Captain stepped forward. "We're here to escort you and Alex Cave to an urgent World Council meeting."

When the Captain stepped aside, Jadin and Alex followed the Sargent out of the building to a waiting police airplane, then climbed into the back seat before the Sargent got in and closed the door. A moment later, it took off and headed toward the IC.

***

INDUSTRIAL CITY COURTHOUSE. WORLD GOVERNMENT COUNCIL MEETING.:

Alex looked out the window at the airport as the plane landed in front of the terminal. He and Jadin climbed out and got into a police vehicle then were driven to a three-story stone structure. The officers let them out, and they were escorted through large glass doors into the foyer.

The Sargent urged them straight across and through a set of wooden doors, and then Alex studied the room. He passed a two person elevated podium, and behind it was a wall of nineteen large monitors with no images on the screens. Directly across from the podium were two wooden desks, each with two chairs.

Alex looked at the Captain, who indicated for them to be seated before he moved away to stand near the exit, so they did as instructed then Alex leaned close to Jadin's ear. "This looks like a courtroom. What happens now?"

"I'm not sure. These don't happen very often and I've only watched one of them on television. It starts when the current local council members, Nathan Palmer and Amanda Cross, come in. We stand up while the other council members appear on the monitors behind them, and that large screen at the end of the room will show the proceedings being sent around the world."

"Essex must have turned us in."

"I doubt it. He's been on our side since I've known him."

Nathan and Amanda entered the room, so Alex and Jadin got up out of their chairs. The images of the other nineteen men and women of the World Council appeared on the monitors behind Amanda and Nathan, and when they sat down, Alex and Jadin did the same.

Alex looked at the single large monitor, and the screen was off. "I guess they're not sharing this with the rest of the planet."

Nathan held up a data storage device. "Tell us who made this recording."

Alex stood up. "I did."

"What you don't understand is that most of your kind volunteered for the procedure. Who doesn't want a long, healthy life?"

Jadin jumped out of her chair. "What about Ms. Donnelly? I know she didn't volunteer."

"We consider what's best for society and take appropriate action when necessary. We give them a chance to volunteer, of course, but some of them resist. Fortunately, central North America is the only place where androids live among flesh and blood humans, or what we call *fleshies*. The rest of the people on this planet are already converted. They all continue to live their lives as before, doing their work and developing new relationships, and enjoying life without the constant worry of dying."

Jadin noticed some of the council members were not very attractive. "If they volunteer, why do they look the same as before? Why not get a beautiful body?"

"That's one of the stipulations. We don't want a planet where everyone looks the same."

"Is that what you have in store for the rest of us?"

"No, Jadin. You and Alex can stay with the rest of the fleshies."

"That's kind of you. I expected to disappear like the rest of the rebels."

"We noticed the trend of rebellion from the people in this region of the planet. That's why we started with the other continents."

Alex thought about his United States and fought hard to hide his smirk. *I'm glad to see some things remain the same.* "Why let us live at all?"

"We need fleshies for our research in genetic manipulation. I'm sure Nora told you about our success in creating geniuses. Donnelly was one of our creations, but she wouldn't cooperate. It seems she preferred being a fleshy. It was difficult because we had to eliminate the memories of her capture, but the transfer was successful."

Alex studied the images on the monitors behind Nathan and Amanda. "I see. We continue being the subjects of your experiments, or we're eliminated."

Amanda looked at Jadin. "Ms. Avery, surely you agree the system here in North America is working, and most of you fleshies don't know the truth. You are well cared for and live happy lives. What more does a society need?"

"Our lives are not so happy while we live in fear. Why do you hunt us?"

"Long ago, we learned fleshies get too bored in a perfect society. This system gives you a sense of adventure and purpose in your otherwise boring lives."

Alex knew they were hiding important information and had an idea what it might be, so he stared at Amanda and Nathan. "Do either of you daydream at all?"

Jadin saw the change in their expressions while they hesitated to reply, which meant the human consciousness was in complete control. "It appears Nora did a magnificent job, transferring your minds into mechanical bodies. The problem is, without being able to daydream, you cannot be creative. That's why you need flesh and blood humans. If we don't create ideas for you, your utopian society will stagnate."

Amanda got up and strolled to the front of the desk to look at Jadin. "We allow you to use intercourse to create new life because you love breaking the law. The success rate is low, and that's fine with us. It's an interesting experiment to see what type of new DNA abnormality will be created naturally."

Something occurred to Alex. "If you need humans to procreate, why hunt the rebels?"

"Population control."

Alex glared at her. "We're not the only people who know about this meeting, and if something happens to us, the person who has a copy of the recording will share it with the rest of the humans."

Amanda didn't back down. "If you tell them the truth, you'll start a mass panic among the fleshies working next to our mechanical race of humans, and your society will collapse. Our only option will be to eliminate any fleshies who oppose us."

Alex's hands clenched into fists. "Will you please stop calling us fleshies?"

"What should we call you?"

Alex considered the question for a moment. "Refer to us as people."

Amanda studied Alex's eyes, and something about them seemed different from the other fleshies on this planet. "You're not from around here, are you?"

Jadin covered for him. "Of course he is. I'm sure you've checked his records."

Amanda smirked at her. "Right. So, how should we let this play out, Jadin? On one hand, you show the recording to the rest of the people, knowing if we go to war, you don't have a chance of defeating us. Or keep letting them live in relative peace?"

"I need to speak with someone before I can answer that question."

"You mean Alex's nephew, Derek. The leader of the rebellion. Of course. You're free to leave and catch a cylinder back to your base of operations. We'll meet you here again in twenty-four hours. I trust you don't need a police escort."

When the screens went dark and the council members left the room, Alex saw the Sargent indicate for him and Jadin to leave. He followed her out of the building, grateful to still be a free man. Well, almost, since he was still stuck in this strange reality.

It was a short walk to the entrance of the underground transportation system, where he saw Jadin swipe her PDSD over a scanner to pass through the rotating bars. A knot formed in his stomach when he realized he would need to scan his data device to pass through the security gate. He held his breath, hoping the computer couldn't tell the difference between him and the real Alex then passed his device over the scanner. He heard a buzzer then pushed on the bar, relieved when it moved then he entered the structure.

Jadin turned in time to see Alex grinning as he passed through the gate. She looped her arm around his before heading down the stairs onto the main platform. Dozens of people were getting out of cylinders on the far side of the large station, while on her side, people were waiting for the cylinders to arrive. She couldn't help studying each one for a clue to whether they were a machine or flesh and blood.

She looked up at Alex, who was studying the display for the travel system. "The colors indicate the destinations of the arriving cylinders."

"Can the council detect if we change where we go?"

"Normally they wouldn't bother, but yeah, they'll be tracking our PDSD's."

Alex watched a cylinder arrive and stop. The door opened, but no one got in then Jadin tugged on his arm, so he followed her over and they got inside. She swiped her device, and the door closed then they sat down and the cylinder gained speed.

She looked at Alex and saw his perplexed expression. "Only authorized people can get a ride to Essex's base. Evidently, none of those people work there."

A few minutes later, the cylinder slowed down and stopped at the terminal near the fabrication hangar. Three people were waiting to get in as they stepped out then Jadin turned to study them. She received curious stares in return and looked away, grabbing Alex's arm and leading him out of the room to the street.

"This is maddening, not being able to tell friend from foe."

She saw four empty vehicles parked in front of the building and climbed into the nearest one.

Once Alex was beside her, she backed up and headed down the road.

Alex was familiar enough to know they were not headed to her robotics lab. "What's going on?"

"We need to tell Essex what happened in the meeting before we go to Derek."

"If he turned us in, he already knows what's happening."

"You're wrong. He's dedicated his life to leaving the WG."

Jadin stopped the vehicle in front of John's office and climbed out, not waiting for Alex as she hurried through the doorway. She stopped at the security desk and looked down the hallway through the glass door, and saw John sitting at his desk.

John saw Alex and Jadin at the security desk and leapt out of his chair then threw open the door and raced down the hallway to Jadin. "I've been worried about what happened to you. Jim Coburn called me when a police airplane landed near your lab and took you away. I called the Police Captain to find out why, but he said it was WG business and wouldn't elaborate."

Alex wondered why Coburn hadn't stopped the police from arresting them, and then remembered he still didn't know the intricacies of this society. Especially under the current circumstances. Perhaps in this reality, Coburn was an android.

John led them down the hallway and through the door into his office, and then indicated for them to sit down as he moved around to his own chair and did the same. "Where did they take you, Jadin?"

"To a secret council meeting. Guess what? We are the only humans left on the entire planet."

Jadin told him everything that had happened. "We're on our way to talk to Derek about this, and I wanted your opinion."

John took a moment to consider the situation. "They haven't stopped me from colonizing Mars, so make sure part of the agreement must be to make it strictly for humans."

"What about the rest of us who don't want to live underground on a lifeless planet?"

"Now that I know the truth, I don't think you should tell the others just yet. I know I hate being someone's experiment, too, and so will many of the rebels. In fact, I wish I didn't know the truth. My life was far less complicated than it is now."

Jadin looked over at Alex. "What do you think?"

He stared across the desktop. "I agree with you, John. Sorry, Mister Essex. It's an old habit. Those who feel like rats in an experiment will want to fight to regain their freedom. Unlike you, in my reality, there is always a war, so I know how it will end. Thousands will die, and those who survive will be put into camps. It's a no-win situation for humanity."

"How much does your nephew know?"

"Only that some of us are being converted into androids, and that we can't tell them apart."

Alex got up from the chair and decided to test John's loyalty. "We'd better get going. I'm sure he's already telling his close friends and we need to stop him. Do you want to see Cave City?"

John jumped out of his seat, waving his hands no. "I don't want to know. If things don't work out, I'm not going to be the reason the police find it. No. You two get going and do some damage control. You know where to find me."

Jadin got out of her chair. "All right, Mr. Essex. I'll let you know how things turn out."

John stared after Alex and Jadin until they left the building then plopped down onto his chair and stared out the window. He knew the last thing humans need right now is a war.

Chapter 24

THE CAVE:

When Alex reached the boulder, one of the two young men guarding the trail recognized him. "Derek says to let you and your friends through, Mister Cave."

"It's nice to be trusted."

When Alex placed his palm on the boulder, the holopath magically appeared and he led the way along the trail, followed by Jadin and Seti then turned and walked backward for a moment to face Jadin. "I forgot to ask if you had clearance to come here."

"No, this is my first time to Cave City. Working for Essex has its drawbacks. I couldn't take the chance of being interrogated if I got caught."

Alex turned around and continued along the trail. At the end of the path, he touched the large tree, and then the tunnel appeared. He hurried inside and asked a woman to tell Derek his uncle was here then entered the garden with the ladies.

Jadin looked around at the lush foliage before sitting on one of the wooden benches. "This is nice."

Alex noticed a handsome young man enter the room and did a double take when he realized it was his nephew. "Wow. You sure look different."

Jadin got off the bench and smiled at the beardless man with a haircut. "You clean up nice."

Derek smiled at her, and then looked at Seti. "What do you think?"

Seti studied Derek for a moment. "I thought you looked fine as you were."

She saw Derek's smile slipping away. "Now you look more intelligent."

It wasn't the answer he expected, and Derek wondered why she was not attracted to him. His thoughts were interrupted by Jadin's voice, so he turned to look at her. "What was that?"

"I said Alex and I were arrested and taken to a secret council meeting. We flesh and blood humans are on the verge of extinction."

Derek had a sinking feeling in his stomach and led everyone into the meeting room. "How many androids are there? I guess that's the wrong question. How many of us flesh and blood humans are left on this planet?"

"Exactly three-thousand. All here in central North America."

Derek slowly sat on a chair and stared at a vase of flowers on the table to gather his thoughts then looked up at Jadin. "How can we stop them?"

Jadin pulled out a chair and sat down to look into his eyes. "We can't. The council offered a deal that works for both sides."

Derek listened to Jadin's explanation that he was just an experiment, and his hands clenched into fists on his knees. When she told him about the agreement with the WC, his hands slowly relaxed.

"You said they won't stop us from having natural births. I can live with that issue. What about Ms. Donnelly? Are they going to force people to become droids?"

"I'm afraid so, but only very intelligent ones. They'll give them a chance to volunteer to have a mechanical body, but if they refuse, they'll be forced to undergo the procedure."

"I feel like someone's pet."

"I know, but what choice do we have?"

"I'm tired of being a wanted criminal. Hell, I might eventually get an android body just so my life is simpler. I don't want to be in charge. I never did."

He looked at Alex. "Better yet. I'll leave with you in your spaceship."

Jadin grabbed Derek's arm to get his attention. "Right now we need to decide if telling three-thousand people what's going on is the right thing to do. They made it clear any rebels who fight back will be eliminated immediately. We can't win, and Alex said our lives will become a real living hell. He knows what he's talking about. How many people have you told about the incident with Ms. Donnelly?"

Derek realized Jadin was correct. "Just Maria. She felt the same way as you about telling everyone what happened. Now I agree with all of you. I don't want to tell three-thousand people they live in a giant terrarium for a race of androids."

"In twenty-three hours, Alex and I will inform the council."

Alex knew he needed to dash Derek's hope of going with him in his spaceship. "How long will it take you to get there using your transportation system?"

Derek wondered what Alex was getting at. "It's a four-hour walk to the nearest tube station. Why do I need to go?"

"Because the council already recognizes you as the rebel leader."

"All right, but I sure as hell didn't ask for the job."

"Good. Jadin, I'll give you a ride back to the base, and then I'm going down to the lab."

Jadin didn't like the idea of leaving Alex's side. "I'll go with you until the meeting."

"Not this time. Seti and I have some work to do."

"Are you going to try the experiment?"

"Not yet."

"Okay. I suppose you want me to tell Essex about the decision."

"That would be great. Thanks for offering."

Jadin and Derek followed Alex and Seti out of the room and stared after them until they entered the tunnel then Jadin sat on a bench. "I think he is going to leave this reality."

"I hope not. I like him a lot better than the original."

"Yeah, me too."

$$***$$

THE LAB:

Alex followed Seti from his ship into the lab. A doorway appeared in the far wall, so they continued into the room and stopped in front of a computer keyboard on a small pedestal. He watched Seti enter a command, and then a holographic screen appeared.

He had no idea what the symbols meant. "Do you have a way to translate the writing into my language so I can understand his experiment?"

"Yes."

The symbols rearranged themselves into the English language and Alex read the information, but didn't understand some of the terminology. "I'm not a physicist, so I guess you'll need to explain what he was doing."

"Drax was obsessed with his experiment, and for years he calculated the physics of black holes, confident it was a way to pass into an alternate reality. The problem is entering fast enough to compensate for the stretching effect of gravity."

"What about this spaceship? Could it enter and withstand the effect?"

"Theoretically, it's possible."

"Drax must have considered that option and tried it. I know I would have."

Seti searched through the data in the computer. "There's only one reference to the ship. That's odd. He made a recording a few moments before he entered the experiment chamber. I'll play it."

Alex saw an elderly man appear on the monitor, but when he spoke, it was not English. "You'll have to translate for me."

"Sorry about that. He's saying he's about to test a theory. If it works, this ship will swap places with one in a parallel universe."

She turned to look up at Alex. "He never mentioned using the ship to the rest of us. When he disappeared inside the chamber, we figured the experiment worked, so the rest of the scientists went to different destinations to improve the odds of surviving."

"I'm no physicist, but I don't think the ship idea worked. If his theory was correct, my laboratory with the virtual copy of you should have followed me into this one. Why didn't you and this ship end up in my reality?"

"I don't know."

"Did he mention any research into returning to a previous location?"

"No. He wasn't worried about that problem. According to his notes, he could not control which reality he would enter."

Alex saw a chair and plopped down onto the cushion. "Anyway I look at it, I can't choose a destination. It may not work at all, or I might disappear into oblivion."

Seti turned to him and smiled. "No. We know it works, because you're proof of that aspect of the experiment."

"But we don't know what will happen to the Alex I trade places with, who will suddenly be thrown into this reality."

"It sounds like you're finding excuses to stay in this one."

"No, I'm not. I can't live in a socialistic society where androids are in charge of my future. It is the reality experiment, or you, Melvin, and I head out into the galaxy."

"I like the second option much better than the first one. I don't want you to leave me here among these droids."

Melvin's voice came through the intercom. "Alex, I feel the same as Seti. I was looking forward to some exciting new adventures with you. I like Jadin, too."

Seti placed her hand on Alex's arm. "I'm feeling a strange emotion. I like Jadin, but the idea of her traveling with us irritates me."

"It's called jealousy. To be honest, when I touch her, it's like she's draining my energy. I've been more tired than usual, too. You said something about my aura being different from the humans living in this reality. Is that still true?"

"Yes, and I've been monitoring your condition. Your aura is slowly getting darker, and now that you've told me how you feel, I believe this entire reality is slowly draining your life-force."

Alex slowly stood up and looked at the empty chamber. "It seems I don't have a choice. I'll go to the surface first and say goodbye to Jadin and Derek. Do you want to come with me?"

"Of course. I won't come down here without Melvin to get me back to the surface. I guess it will just be me and him after you try the experiment."

"What about Derek and Jadin? Can you work with them in this reality?"

"I like Derek, but I feel the same about the androids on this planet as you do. I'd rather head out into the galaxy. Melvin, how do you feel about staying here with Jadin and Derek?"

"From now on, control of what happens to the flesh and blood humans will be up to the androids. There is nothing you and I can do here to help Derek and Jadin, so I say we take them with us to explore the galaxy."

Seti grabbed Alex's hand. "I will miss you. On the bright side, I'm not jealous of Jadin joining our team."

"Good. I was hoping you'd take care of them for me. How will you deal with the new version of Alex?"

"It depends on how he reacts when he arrives."

"Okay. Let's get started."

***

CAVE CITY:

Derek and Jadin noticed Alex and Seti entering the main chamber and got up from a bench. Derek ran his fingers through his hair as they hurried over to greet them then he smiled at Seti. "That was fast. Is there a change of plan?"

Alex looked around at the curious expressions of the seventeen people lounging on the grass and benches. "Yes. Let's go outside to talk."

Derek and Jadin indicated they agreed and followed them out through the tunnel. "What's going on?"

"I've discovered I have no choice in the path I choose. If I stay in this reality, I'll die. My only option is to use the alternate reality experiment and try to get home."

Derek's heart sank into his stomach. "You just came into my life. Are you positive?"

Alex gave him a solemn nod he was. "I'm sorry, Derek. This might make you feel better. Seti and Melvin want you and Jadin to join them in exploring the galaxy."

Derek's heart rate increased. "Is this a joke? Because I hope not."

Seti grinned at Derek's enthusiasm. "It's true. Just don't tell anyone about us."

Derek quickly scanned the area to make sure they were alone. "Right. Wait a minute. How am I going to explain my sudden disappearance?"

"You and Jadin need to work that out."

Jadin wasn't about to give up. "If you leave this solar system, won't that change the effect it's having on you?"

"It won't make a difference, because I'll still be in this reality. No, I have no choice but to leave."

Jadin looked into Alex's eyes. "I'm going to miss this version of you."

"What are you going to tell the real version if he returns?"

"I'm not waiting to find out. I don't want to wait around here, and the Mars colony mission still needs to be done, no matter the current circumstances. Those are real people up there, and we can't abandon them on that rock, so I'm going to help them first."

Derek reached out to shake hands, and then remembered what happens. "I guess this is goodbye."

"I suppose it is. I may not be your real uncle, but I'm proud of what you've accomplished in this reality. Have fun on your adventures."

"I appreciate this opportunity, and I hope you find what you're looking for, Alex."

"Thanks."

Alex touched the tree, and then the holopath appeared. He gave a final nod of good luck to Derek, and then he and Seti headed back to the clearing.

Chapter 25

THE LAB:

Alex moved over next to Seti, and when she looked up at him, saw the anguish in her eyes. "What's wrong?"

"I don't understand why I feel this way about you. I didn't feel this sad when the others left."

"Perhaps it's because now you know what it's like to be alone for millions of years."

"That's not it. This is what I imagined heartbreak would feel like."

The look in her eyes tore at his heart, and he was relieved when the ship entered the water. He headed over to the control console to look at the blank screen as the ship headed for the seafloor. When he looked back at Seti, she made eye contact without speaking to him, and then headed down to the cargo hold. A few minutes later, the illuminated docking hole appeared on the screen and the ship dropped into the opening.

He headed down the stairs, glancing into the living area before reaching the bottom. He saw the entrance into the lab through the airlock windows then the doors opened and he led the way through into the main area.

Seti opened the entrance to the parallel universe experiment, and then led Alex inside. She indicated the chamber, and a light came on inside the small room. Alex approached the entrance and stopped before stepping inside. He leaned in and saw a small control on the left wall, but no concave screen or hand controls, like in the time viewer.

He leaned back out and looked at Seti. "Do I control it from inside? Or is it done on the other console?"

"It can be activated by either. Just press the red button. If you prefer, I can do it for you from out here."

"I think I can handle it. Well. I guess this is it."

"Would you mind if I give you a hug?"

Alex smiled and held out his arms. "Of course not."

Seti wrapped her arms around his neck and held him close while leaning her head against his cheek. She fought to rein in her emotions, but lost the battle and let her tears flow.

Alex felt Seti's warm body against his for the first time since they met, and now her tears were running down his neck. She seemed so human it broke his heart he couldn't stay, and then he had an idea. "I want you to come with me."

Seti let go and wiped away her tears with the back of her hands then looked into his eyes. "The thing is, we theorized perhaps an android as advanced as I am cannot be transported to a parallel universe. That's part of the reason I stayed behind."

"You said it was just a theory, so the worst that happens is you remain in the chamber when I leave. I'm willing to take the chance."

Melvin's voice came from the speaker system. "What about Jadin and Derek?"

"That depends on you. If this works, Seti and I will be replaced by our alternates. You'll need to decide if you like them or not."

"That's the nice part about being a spaceship. If I don't like the new versions of you and Seti, I'll get the kids and leave this planet."

"Thanks. Goodbye, my friend. You should shut the airlock doors in case something goes wrong."

"I will. Goodbye, Alex."

Alex reached out from the chamber. "Take my hand and step in, and let's see what happens."

Once she entered the room, he held his hand over the red button. "Here we go."

Alex pressed it, and the door closed then he was nearly blinded by a flash of brilliant white light. He blinked a few times and saw the door was open, and then felt Seti's hand in his. "Did it work?"

"I don't know. I don't feel any different."

"I'll try my implant to contact the virtual Seti in this reality."

He reached up to his right ear and touched the device. "Seti, this is Alex. Can you hear me?"

He looked over at Seti, who indicated she heard him without speaking, and then waited a few more moments, but nothing happened. "You must have traded places with this version. That's a relief. She was a little psychotic."

Alex led Seti out of the chamber, expecting to see Jadin waiting for him, but the room was empty and the exit was closed. "Seti, can you tell if Melvin is out there?"

"Yes, I'm in contact with him, and his operating system seems the same."

Alex saw the exit appear and the closed airlock door. "Melvin, can you hear me?"

"I'm here, Alex. I don't believe the experiment worked."

"I guess there is only one way to find out. Let us in and we'll head to the surface to see if anything is different."

The airlock doors opened and Alex led Seti into the cargo hold, and then closed the airlock before she closed the entrance into the lab. They hurried up the stairs into the dimly lit control room, neither wanting to sit down until they knew if it worked or not.

A few moments later, sunlight filled the room as the ship burst from the ocean and gained altitude. Alex saw the string of Aleutian Islands, all with much lower shorelines. As they climbed higher, the cloudless sky allowed him to see sprawling structures spaced along the coast of the Pacific Ocean.

He dropped to his knees and closed his eyes, and then a tear ran down his cheek. "I'm home."

A thought suddenly occurred to him, and he jumped up from the floor. "Melvin, can you determine what year this is?"

"I cannot."

"Take us to Essex's base and we'll check in with Jadin and Okawna."

Alex stared at the landscape rushing past three-thousand feet beneath the ship, but he didn't recognize the cities below. Several minutes later, the ship lost altitude and dropped toward a different-looking base.

"Melvin, are you sure this is Essex's facility?"

"Yes, this is the same location as in the other reality."

"Okay, let's land behind his office."

The ship set down on the lawn and they hurried down the stairs and out of the airlock, and then headed across the grass toward John's living quarters. "Seti, why don't you wait here until I know what's going on?"

***

John noticed something in his peripheral vision and looked to find out what it was, and then his jaw dropped open when he recognized the man in front of him. "Alex? Where did you come from?"

"The lab. Two days ago, I was sent to an alternate reality, and I just learned how to get back."

"That was six years ago, Alex. You came back a few moments after you entered the time viewer, but you had been shot in the head. It caused a brain injury, and you lost your memory. You murdered a guard then shot and killed Okawna. You tried to shoot Sam, and he accidentally shot and killed Jadin before Coburn killed you."

Alex stared at John for a long moment while dealing with the realization his friends were dead, and then eased onto one of the chairs. "That wasn't me. That was the Alex from the alternate reality. I guess we did trade places."

John looked away from Alex when a lovely young woman suddenly entered from his living quarters. "Who are you, and how did you get in here?"

Alex turned and realized Seti had joined them then got up. "John, this is my friend from the alternate reality. Her name is Seti. She's not like the holograph we saw in the lab. They traded places."

When she had Alex's attention, Seti indicated for him to use his implant as she smiled at John to keep his attention. "Alex speaks highly of you."

Alex touched the tiny red button. *"What's up?"*

"Alex, he's an android, like in my reality."

Alex turned his head to hide his astonishment. *"What about the rest of the people on the base?"*

"I'm sensing only androids."

Alex realized he needed to be careful about what he said. "John, you haven't aged a bit since I left. In fact, you look younger."

"A lot has happened since you died. I mean, went away. Do you remember the androids I sent on a deep space mission? Well, they came back with some great ideas and we've implemented them into our new society. I had my consciousness uploaded into this android body, and now I'll live forever and explore the galaxy."

"That's great, John. Will I be able to get an android body?"

"I'm afraid not. Legally, you're dead."

"That's okay. I'll live with the rest of the flesh and blood people. I'm sure they have a different philosophy about life. Sure, your new body thinks, speaks, and acts like you, but is the *original you* still alive in there? Or are you just a copy?"

John hesitated to answer. "It doesn't matter anymore. Everyone has optioned for the conversion, and you are the last flesh and blood person on the planet."

"I see. What happens now?"

"I'm not sure. I'll let the authorities know you've returned, and we'll find out."

"He's lying, Alex. I can read its thoughts, and there are hundreds of real people in a work camp. That's what he has planned for us. Security droids are almost here."

"All right, John. Do you mind if I use your toilet?"

"Since we don't need them, they've been removed."

"No problem. I'll go outside."

When Alex headed for the side door, John saw Seti following him and thought they must be more than friends. When they disappeared around the corner of the building, he suddenly remembered Melvin and ran to the door. He raced around to his backyard and saw Alex standing inside the airlock, so he hurried over to him.

"Wait! Where are you going?"

"I'm not sure. Jadin and Okawna are dead, and I'm not living in a society of androids. Goodbye, John."

Alex closed the doors and ran up the stairs to the control room then looked down at John as the ship gained altitude. A vehicle stopped at the corner of the building and four armed guards got out, scanning the area until John went over and joined them.

Seti moved over beside Alex. "This reality is similar to the one we left. Essex didn't know I'm also an android and was going to put us in the camp with the other humans to diversify the gene pool."

"I wonder if this will happen every time I use the experiment. Melvin, take us to the lab. I'll use the time viewer to see what happens if I try again."

"I could do that, Alex, but I'm curious about the human camp. Let's check it out before we go."

Alex would prefer not to go because he knew if he saw people suffering, he would want to help them. He also knew it would be a lost cause and hundreds of humans would die.

"Melvin, you're part of this team, so if it's important to you, we'll go. But to be honest, I don't think we should get involved with their system. I know it won't end well."

"It's not that important, Alex. I'll take us to the lab."

Seti got Alex's attention. "I heard your thoughts. Now I know why your original team trusted you."

Alex reached up and turned off the implant. "I forgot about it."

***

Alex stepped into the time viewing chamber and turned to smile at Seti. "I'll be back in a moment."

He turned around and placed his hands on the control pads, and the door closed. The indigo light filled the room, and then the screen showed colored lights streaming out from the center. He concentrated on stepping into the parallel universe experiment and the chamber appeared on the screen, showing him and Seti entering and the door closing. The door immediately opened, and he saw himself and Seti stepping out.

He focused his thoughts on Jadin, and the screen showed her working in her lab. She appeared to be moving in fast motion, but he recognized a few pieces of the equipment she used for her brain transfer experiment. He saw a person's arm aiming a pistol at Jadin's head. The gun fired, and the arm disappeared then he saw himself kneeling on the floor, cradling her in his arms.

Alex let go of the buttons, but just before the screen went dark, he saw Derek's image staring back at him, aiming the gun at his own head then white light entered the room as the door opened.

Seti saw the fear in Alex's eyes as he stepped out of the chamber. "What did you see?"

"You and I used the experiment and went to a reality further back in time. Jadin was working on the early stages of her experiment, and someone shot her."

"Was it you?"

"I don't think so. In that reality, Jadin didn't finish her work, and the androids were never built, so that society would all be flesh and blood humans. We need to use the experiment again. Now that I know there are realities where the populations are normal, I believe if I keep trying, we'll eventually find a permanent place to stay."

"You keep saying we. Does that include Melvin?"

"Of course. I believe your inventor friend was correct about using the laboratory ship to pass through a black hole. That's why the three of us didn't notice the change in realities. Let's use the experiment unless you want to stay here."

Seti took Alex by the hand and led him out into the main room then opened the entrance to the parallel universe experiment. "I'm ready when you are."

Alex gave her hand a light squeeze, and then they stepped into the chamber. The door closed, and white light filled the room.

The end.

Movie script available from the author.

I hope you enjoyed Parallel. Please take a moment to write a short review. Thank you.
James M. Corkill

Here is a preview of the next book by this author.

Eruption

Chapter 1

NORTH AMERICA. SAN DIEGO, CALIFORNIA:

Marcus Hunter was standing on the dock beside his one-hundred-foot motorsailer named *Windancer*, ready to head out to a small harbor on the southern coast of Peru. He scratched the stubble of his beard as he looked down at his fourteen-year-old granddaughter, Geneva Hunter, who was ignoring him while texting. The last time he saw her, she was six years old and four feet tall, but now she was five foot nine and still growing.

He looked up and smiled when he saw his forty-three-year-old daughter, Doctor Olivia Hunter, strolling along the dock while pulling a large suitcase on wheels. Beside her was her eighteen-year-old daughter, Rickie Hunter, who was also pulling a suitcase.

Olivia stopped and gave Marcus a hug. "Hi, Dad. It's good to see you again."

"It's good to see you, too."

When everyone had their backs to her, Geneva looked up from her phone to study her long-lost relatives. She recognized her cousin from the funeral, but seemed shorter than she remembered. As Olivia turned and stared at her, she stopped breathing and quickly turned away, then began texting her girlfriend in Reno while trying to get rid of the knot in her stomach.

Rickie wondered what had caused Geneva's stunned reaction to seeing her aunt, then she turned to Marcus and wrapped her arms around his neck for a quick hug. "Hi, Grandpa. I'm looking forward to this new adventure."

Rickie stepped back and studied her cousin, who was ignoring her while still texting. They grew up in different sides of society, and she had not seen Geneva in eight years. She studied the tattoo of a three-headed snake on Geneva's right arm, not sure what to expect from the young girl from Reno, Nevada. All she knew was Geneva had spent more time on the streets than at home with her other grandparents. "Hey, Cuz. I doubt you remember me."

When Geneva ignored her and continued texting, Rickie turned to her grandfather. "How soon can we leave?"

"As soon as you and Geneva take in the mooring lines."

Marcus grabbed Rickie's suitcase, then he and Olivia went across the gangway up onto his ship and disappeared below deck. Rickie removed the spring line, coiling the rope over her arm and cinching it closed with a loop before tossing it onto the deck. When she noticed Geneva still texting, she moved in front of her, then folded her arms across her chest. "Are you going to help me?"

Geneva didn't look up. "I'm not a sailor, so I don't know what to do. I'm sure you can handle it."

Rickie snatched the phone from Geneva's hand and held it out over the water. "I'm glad you're offering to help me by releasing that stern line."

Geneva's hands clenched into fists at her sides as she glared at Rickie. "Give me my phone or I swear I'll kill you!"

Even though they were nearly the same height, Rickie was not intimidated and slid the phone into her back pocket. "Not yet. You need to earn the right to use it on our trip."

Geneva was surprised her intimidation expression wasn't working on her cousin, who she barely remembered. She caught movement in her peripheral vision, but continued glaring at Rickie. "Fine with me. I didn't want to go on this stupid boat trip in the first place. Give me my phone and I'm out of here."

When Marcus stepped out onto the main deck, he saw the girls down on the dock, staring at each other. "What's the holdup?"

Rickie continued locking stares with her cousin. "Nothing, Grandpa. We're just getting to know each other."

Geneva broke eye contact to look up at Marcus on the ship. "She said I don't have to go with you, so I'm going to get my stuff and go home."

Rickie pulled the phone from her pocket, smiling as she held it out to Geneva. "Don't forget your pacifier."

Geneva glared at Rickie as she snatched the phone from her hand, then slid it into her pocket as she stomped across the gangway onto the ship. She stopped at the top and looked at Rickie, who was still smiling at her, then she gave her the finger before disappearing below deck to pack her belongings.

Rickie looked up at Marcus. "I got this. Start the engines and let's get going before she gets her stuff."

Marcus grinned and hurried into the pilothouse, then started the engines driving the generators for the electric motor driven propellers. When Rickie ran up the gangway and began stowing it into a bracket, he engaged the thrusters to silently move the *Windancer* away from the dock. Once clear of the other ships, he rotated the thrusters to move the *Windancer* forward into the harbor.

***

Geneva shoved the last of her clothes into a large backpack, then shoved a fresh pack of cigarettes into her shirt pocket. She left her cabin and hurried up the stairs to the main deck, then froze in place when she realized they were in the middle of the harbor.

She tossed her backpack onto the deck, then stomped up the outside stairs into the pilothouse. She kept her clenched fists at her side as she glared at the back of Marcus, who was sitting in a captain's chair at the helm, and Rickie facing her from the chair next to him. "Take me back to the dock or I'll jump over the side and swim back!"

When Rickie smirked at her, Geneva moved over to the other chair next to Marcus, but didn't sit down. "Did you hear what I said?"

Marcus looked over at her. "I'm sorry, but I can't leave you alone on the mainland."

"I can take care of myself."

"I'm sure you can, but now you're my responsibility. This will be a good opportunity for all of us to get to know each other."

"By bobbing around on the water? No thanks. I'm leaving."

Rickie waited until Geneva was about to step outside. "Don't forget your pacifier doesn't like salt water."

Geneva stopped and spun around. "I'll put it in a baggie."

"If you look out the window, you'll see it's a long swim to shore."

Geneva glared at them until Olivia came up the inside stairs. She avoided looking at her aunt as she headed out of the pilothouse and down the steps onto the main deck.

Marcus smiled when his two girls were sitting in the captain's chairs on both sides of him as he continued out into open water. When he turned south and the traffic thinned out, he raised the automated sails and they bellowed full of wind. The speed quickly increased as he shut down the engines, and the only sound was the whisper of the wind through the open side windows.

He looked out the front window, where Geneva was lying on a recliner in the shade of the white mainsail. She was the only child of his son, Thomas, who had been an aviation mechanic in the United States Air Force. When he was killed in combat eight years ago, her mother became an alcoholic and died when she crashed her car six months later. Geneva was raised by her mother's elderly grandparents, who were living on social security in Reno.

When he learned she was getting into trouble, he thought going on an adventure with her family would be good for her, but she refused to leave. He had filed for custody and won, then yesterday he had flown to Reno to get her, even though she fiercely protested leaving her friends.

Olivia reached into a small refrigerator and grabbed a bottle of beer, then handed it to her father. "It's great to be on the water again."

Marcus grinned as he took the bottle and swallowed some of the cool liquid. "I'm glad to see you getting away from the city for a while. All the stress you put on yourself worrying about your patients isn't good for your mental health."

"I can't help it. Even now, I worry about some of the worst cases. I'm hoping this trip will help me forget about them for a while."

"It usually does."

Olivia looked past Marcus to see Rickie. "Do either of you know why Geneva is avoiding me?"

Rickie shrugged her shoulders. "No, but I think she's mad at all of us."

Marcus knew better. "I'm the one she's mad at for dragging her away from her friends. You're both just collateral damage."

Rickie leaned back in her chair. "Once we stop at our first foreign port, I'll take her in to town and she'll get over it."

"Thanks. I think you'll be good for her."

"Not that I'm too worried, Grandpa, but what kind of trouble did she get into in Reno that was so bad?"

"According to the police report, a man had her arrested for pulling a knife on him in the park and demanding money. She claimed he tried to rape her, but there were no witnesses to either claim. The judge dismissed the charges against her for attempted robbery with a weapon, but did not charge the man with attempted rape. I realized she needed someone to understand what she's going through, and who better than my two girls?"

Rickie looked out through the front window and down onto the deck at her cousin. "We'll try."

Award-winning author James M. Corkill is a Veteran, and retired Federal Firefighter from Washington State, USA. He was an electronic technician and studied mechanical engineering in his spare time before eventually becoming a firefighter for 32-years and retiring. He has since settled into the Appalachian Mountains of western North Carolina, and has a fantastic view from his writing desk.

He began writing in 1997, and was fortunate to meet a famous horror writer named Hugh B. Cave, who became his mentor. In 2002, he rushed to self-published a dozen copies of Dead Energy so his wife could see his book published before she was taken by cancer. When his soul mate was gone, he stopped writing and began drinking heavily.

His favorite quote. "When you wake up in the morning, you never know where the day will take you."

In 2013, he met a stranger who recognized his name and had enjoyed an old copy of Dead Energy, except for the ending. When she encouraged him to start writing again, he realized this chance meeting was just what he needed to hear at the right moment. He quit drinking and began the rewrite of Dead Energy into The Alex Cave Series, and thankful for that fateful encounter.

You can contact him at
Jamesmcorkill@gmail.com

I hope you enjoyed Parallel. Please take a
moment to write a short review. Thank you.
James M. Corkill

Other books by James M. Corkill

Dead Energy. The Alex Cave Series Book 1.
Cold Energy. The Alex Cave Series Book 2.
Red Energy. The Alex Cave Series book 3.
Gravity. The Alex Cave Series book 4.
Pandora's Eyes. The Alex Cave Series book
5.
DNA. The Alex Cave Series book 6.
Eruption.

Made in the USA
Columbia, SC
23 November 2024

46704718R00174